Devil In The Bedroom

Devil In The Bedroom

JP Storm

Copyright © 2021 by JP Storm.

Library of Congress Control Number:		2021910070
ISBN:	Hardcover	978-1-6641-7566-2
	Softcover	978-1-6641-7565-5
	eBook	978-1-6641-7564-8

Print information available on the last page.

Rev. date: 05/19/2021

To order additional copies of this book, contact:
Xlibris
844-714-8691
www.Xlibris.com
Orders@Xlibris.com
775853

*The story you are about to read
only the names were changed.*

Prologue

I was awakened by a faint scream of "Momm . . . mie!" so I sat up in bed and heard it again, "Momm . . . mie!" I ran up the stairs and was shocked by what I was seeing.

I could not believe that my child was lying on the floor with her head bobbing up and down.

I kept thinking where all that black stuff was coming from, not realizing it was blood. I must have stood there for a minute or two, but it seemed like hours had passed as I watched Dillon continue to strike Sky, and with each blow, her head would come up off the floor and back down.

As if in a dreamlike state, I snapped out of it and realized this was no dream—he was killing my child.

I screamed at him, "Stop hitting her! Get off her! Leave my house!"

He slowly turned around and looked at me and said in a calm voice, "Oh, so where am I supposed to go?"

I replied, "I do not care, but you have to get out now."

Dillon started walking away, and halfway down the hall, he turned around and came back into the room. As I was kneeling to check on my daughter, he grabbed me from behind and threw me behind Sky, which caused me to break the mirrored closet door.

I remembered I bounced from the shattered glass of the closet and hit my head on the edge of the nightstand. I could hear Sky quietly saying," Stop! Do not hurt my mom."

Once I realized she was coherent, I gently nudged her with my foot and said, "Run if you can and do not look back. I will be okay. I'll find you."

I looked up and saw him coming back, stepping over Sky and around the bed with a ceramic lamp, wrapping the cord around the base. I was thinking, *What is he doing? The bulb is still in there.*

Then he hit me with the base of the lamp.

He kept hitting me saying, "I am not going anywhere." He kept hitting me till the base of the lamp shattered. He took the part of the base with the bulb and struck me with it till the bulb broke. At that moment, I realized I could no longer see out my left eye.

I am getting ahead of myself so let me start at the beginning of how Sky and Dillon came to be.

Chapter One

Sky was a beautiful young black woman of Indian descent with long black hair, fair complexion, and piercing black eyes.

On this particular hot day, she had on a white and navy-blue summer dress, matching heels, hat, and gloves. The way she would dress caused people to stop and stare as her attire was from the fifties and sixties era, and that became her signature look.

She was dating her best friend Jasper, whom she had known since high school. In my opinion he was a handsome young man that I knew for sure was the one she would someday marry. They appeared so much in love - that is until Dillon came along.

She had just finished visiting with friends in the Crenshaw area and was standing at the corner waiting for the light to change when a black stretch limo drove up and stopped.

As she was crossing the street, she heard someone yelling "Hey you! Hey you!"

Sky kept walking, thinking to herself, *He could not be talking to me.* When the light changed, the limo made a U-turn and came upon the side of the street where her car was parked.

As she unlocked the car door, a man got out of the driver side of the limo and opened the back door.

According to Sky, out stepped the most handsome man she had ever seen. He was tall, very well dressed and groomed. His skin was the color of honey, and he wore sunglasses that cost more than what she made in a month. His hair was midnight black, and when he opened his mouth to speak, she knew was hooked.

He stood there in the glistening sun with a beautiful smile, took off his sunglasses, and according to Sky, had the most beautiful piercing blue-green eyes. He held out his hand and introduced himself as Dillon Mason.

She tilted her head to look up at him. With a smile in her voice, she placed her hand in his and replied, "My name is Skylar Grant," and with that being said, he bent to kiss her hand.

Still holding her hand, he said, "That's a beautiful name for a beautiful and stunning young woman. If you're not busy, I would like to take you to lunch and bring you back to your car afterwards."

She was smitten by his good looks, limo, chauffer, the smell of success with a capital **S** and followed him to the limo.

They had lunch, which turned into dinner. After dinner, they were driven around Beverly Hills then to Bel Air to look at the sights. Later, they went to Malibu for drinks and to watch the waves.

Before taking Sky back to her car, he ordered his driver, Gage, to take him to his storage. When Gage got to the gate, he used a remote to open the doors of the storage building, all thirteen of them. Behind twelve of the doors was a car, and behind door 13 was a private plane.

All the cars were *very expensive* and in dark colors—all but one. It was the color of a red tomato, a two-seater Jaguar, the car of her dreams. And there it was right in front of her. She squealed with delight like a kid in a candy store as she got closer and closer to the Jaguar.

Sky learned later Dillon owned the storage facility and everything in it. This storage was only used to house his cars and private plane. This was all new to Sky as she had never seen or experienced anything of this magnitude. She was wondering if a man, one man could possibly own all those.

Sky stood in the storage facility in total awe and, for the first time in her life, was completely speechless. She later told me all the cars looked as though they had been washed and polished, as if, they were show cars on display. He gave her a tour and began telling her what type of cars they were. She had only heard and/or seen cars like that in magazines or Auto Shows. But to be here and this close to all those expensive cars made her feel as though she was dreaming, and yet there she stood with Dillon Mason, owner of twelve cars including her dream car and a private plane.

Seeing how happy she was as they approached the red car, he asked if she would like to drive. You would have thought he said, "Hey, you can have it."

He handed her the keys to the Jaguar, and I can only imagine the smile on her face. Off they went for a drive in the red two-seater Jaguar.

Upon returning to her car, she smiled and became sad all at once. When he asked what was wrong, she replied, "Nothing."

And yet she was sad to be leaving him.

She came home wondering if she would see him again. Would he call or, did she just make him up? She kept saying out loud, "Who has that kind of money? Who looks that good and is not already married to some rich person?"

Just as she thought that out loud, she smiled to herself. God, *thank you for letting me be in the right place at the right time to meet Mr. Dillon Mason who has twelve cars and a plane.*

Sky was a very private person and had only shared her dreams with Jasper and myself of one day owning that very car. She would say, "Once I finish school and secure a great-paying job making at least six figures, I am going to walk into a Jaguar dealership and say, 'I want that one please—yes, the red one on the showroom floor.'

Whenever she spoke of her wanting something, I would tell her to reach for the moon, and you might get what you want. If you do not get the moon, then a star or two will be just fine. But no matter which one you get, always be satisfied and thankful to the good Lord for allowing you to have it.

As Sky was telling me about her meeting and outing with Dillon, I was thinking, *I guess she got the moon and the stars.* Now I am wondering if she was meant to have both at the same time.

Listening to her go on and on about Dillon in my mind, it sounds *to me like he was showing off, to impress a very impressionable young women barley out of twenties. But I continued to listen.*

My instincts as a woman who worked all her life and as a mother warned me something was not right. Something was not rights. Something bad was coming, but I just did not know what or when.

I would tell Sky, "Always appreciate what God has given you, and do not ever think about what others have as you do not know how they obtained them. Just be yourself, and if it is meant to be, you will get yours."

I had a feeling that everything in the storage unit including the plane was leased to Mr. Mason. It was just a feeling, but oh, was the feeling strong.

Over coffee one Saturday, I told my friend La'niece about Dillon and shared my concerns and the bad vibes I was getting from Sky was telling me. Her advice was to pray about and wait and see where this was going.

Things Are Not Always

What

They Appear To Be

CHAPTER TWO

It was not long after their meeting that Dillon had flowers and candy sent to her job every week. They dined at the most extravagant restaurants on a nightly basis, never the same place twice. These were places Sky read about or saw on television but never dreamed she would be there one day. And yet there she was dining nightly and having a great time being with Dillon.

After dinner, they were always driven to various hotel lounges for coffee and dessert.

One thing that was consistently on my mind was when she spoke of Dillon it was always of him, his driver and his business associates. No family or friends was ever mentioned.

Six months had gone by. I became concerned, worried, and suspicious. I had yet to meet this rich man that was dating my daughter and changing her little by little.

He took her shopping in Beverly Hills, spending exorbitant amounts of money on her clothing, shoes, and jewelry. It appears he never liked what she picked out or tried on but would encourage her to try something more to his liking, lifestyle, and approval.

As quickly as he said the words *I do not like*, the clothes he had chosen were in another dressing room waiting for her to try on. And whether she liked them or not, that is what she ended up with and brought home. They were Dillon's choice and his style of what he wanted to see her wearing.

Sky was young and taken in by all the excitement of being able to shop without looking at prices, and quickly became accustomed to his lifestyle.

Red flag, bells and whistles were going off in my head as I listened to what they had done on those shopping days, as she showed me the clothes, shoes, and accessories. She was elated with joy, so I kept quiet and let her be.

On one of her off days, Sky and I were at home in the kitchen having breakfast and discussing this new man, Dillon who came into her like a whirlwind. I was happy that she was happy but always felt there was something about a man who had his own limo, chauffer, who could afford flowers arrangements that cost two to three hundred dollars and took her shopping, it seems like, every other day. I became genuinely concerned because Sky had not introduced me to Dillon.

Why I had this strange feeling I do not know, but I did.

At 8:30 that morning, the doorbell rang. I asked Sky if she was expecting anyone. She shook her head no. I went to the door.

Upon opening the door, there stood this beautiful woman in a navy-blue suit. That suit had to cost fifteen hundred dollars if not more. She had on designer shoes, carried a designer purse and had on a few pieces of very expensive jewelry. She was absolutely stunning.

I finally said, "Yes, may I help you?"

In a very chipper voice, she replied, "Hi, I am Catarina. I am here to see Skylar Grant."

I called Sky.

Once Sky appeared, she introduced herself again and said, "Mr. Mason has paid for my services for the week to be your personal shopper."

"My what?" Again, this time a little louder she said, "My what, and who sent you?"

Catarina repeated that Mr. Mason had paid for her services for the week to pick out her new wardrobe, including evening gowns. She informed

Sky that he was extremely specific about what he wanted and the colors to be chosen.

Also, he had personally selected a hairstylist and makeup artist he wanted her to use as of that day and going forward and that their services had also been paid in advance. Catarina told Sky, "As soon as you get dressed, we could leave and that she would be waiting in the limo."

*   *   *

The weekend was fast approaching, and a messenger was sent to Sky's job with a note from Dillon saying they would be attending a dinner dance in Bel Air. A car would pick her, take her to the hairstylist, makeup artist, and take her home to get dressed, then bring her to Bel Air where he would be waiting. She was instructed to wear one of the gowns he had recently purchased along with the proper shoes and jewelry. She was to contact Catarina should she need help with accessorizing, and Catarina would be there to assist.

So many things were going through my mind, and one thought stood out above the rest: What and who has my child gotten involved with that can just tell her what to wear? To have her hair and makeup done at a moment's notice. Was it because he purchased the clothes and all the other services?

Dillon was creating his own Barbie doll. In my opinion, this was not good. Not good at all.

In my opinion nothing about Dillon Mason was making sense. I did not know him, his world, lifestyle other than he had to look his best and so did Sky when she was with him. I realize as a mother I was being judgmental and did not heed La'niece advice.

Gossip and rumors were starting at her job, and things were becoming bad for Sky. But she did not care. She was happy. She had her "Dillon."

Being in management for several years, I knew how rumors got out of hand, what it could do to her reputation. Eventually it would get all twisted and depending on her manager and the structure of management, it was only a matter of time when she would be dismissed for some reason or some kind of quick policy change put together and approved by upper management. This would for sure be cause for immediate termination of employment.

Yes, Sky thought she was dreaming when she met Dillon, and per Sky, he was constantly telling her there was more to come. "Just be patient, and I will give you the world."

All the time I was thinking, *At what cost, Sky? At what cost?*

*There Is Always a Motive
to What People Do*

When

It's Done for the Wrong Reason

Chapter Three

Sky knew I was anxious to meet Dillon. Without my knowing, she had arranged a meeting that would be taking place soon.

A few days later, at seven forty-five in the evening, the doorbell rang. Standing there was a man I had never seen before dressed in a black suit, white shirt, and tie. I looked down at his shoes, and they were shining like he just took them out of the box. Before he could speak, Sky came down and said, "Mommie, I see you've met Gage."

Gage was one of Dillon's employees who was also his chauffeur.

Looking at Sky, she looked absolutely stunning in a beautiful evening gown of black satin with a matching shawl around her shoulders. Her neck was adorned with a single rope of diamonds, and there were diamond studs on her ears that were just the right size to complement the ones around her neck.

Yes, she was a real-life size doll all dressed up with a limo and chauffeur at her disposal.

As they were leaving, I noticed the neighbors had come outside on the porch and the kids were in the street or sitting on the curb. Everyone, it seemed, was staring at my house. I was thinking how nosy folks became when they see a limousine in our neighborhood. Or were they staring at Sky? Or both?

Gage opened the back door for Sky, and once she was seated and the door closed, he walked around to get in the driver side. That was when I saw the two men on motorcycles in security uniforms behind the limo.

As they were driving away, I was really starting to think who was Dillon Mason? This was a lot to take in as I watched them drive away.

Sky was starting to look as though she belonged in Dillon Mason world. This was not my Sky at all. The person who dressed in vintage clothing and wore hats now looked like she belonged on display.

One Saturday evening I noticed huge garbage bags being brought downstairs, and I wanted to know what was going on. Sky informed me that since Dillon had purchased her a new wardrobe, he insisted she give her other clothes to charity. That meant everything, including her hats, gloves, and shoes. Then she added that I could have her old jewelry to use as I please since I was into crafts, redesign, and sometimes added jewelry to clothes I made.

I wanted to know if that meant she was returning the pieces I had given her for birthdays, and she shook her head yes. I silently took the box she handed me and walked away. The more I thought about all this, the more I knew for sure—this was not good.

Since she was keeping erratic hours, I left a note on her bed and said, "I need to meet Dillon, so make it happen!"

I remembered she had arranged for a meeting, but it was not coming soon enough. That feeling that something was not right continued to nag at me. I wanted to meet the man more than ever and could hardly wait until I did.

I found out a few days later that the event that was to be in Bel Air but was canceled and they flew to San Francisco instead for dinner. She had this smirk look on her face, and I prayed that smirk look was not intended for me.

Now imagine if you will the surprised look I had on my face, and it was not a smirk.

Chapter Four

Because Sky was my only child, I might be overthinking this whole situation and needed to talk to someone that would try to help me make sense of what was going on. So I called Phoenix, my level-headed sister. Up till then, she had no knowledge of all what had taken place as I had given my word not to discuss this newfound relation with anyone, especially Phoenix.

After I finished my second cup of coffee, I made the call. After the fifth ring, she picked up, and I looked toward the ceiling and mouthed, *Thank you.*

I could tell immediately she was running late as usual, but she took a few minutes to hear me out. Those few minutes turned in to thirty minutes then an hour.

I started telling Phoenix I could see little changes that probably no one else noticed. Then significant changes that started a few months into the relationship with Dillon. The hardest change for me was when Sky stopped talking to me in the mornings. Now the most she would say was, "I'll be back in a few days." No *good morning.* No *goodbye.* No *have a great day.* No nothing.

I expressed my concern to Phoenix about the personal shopper, the limo, driver, the security escorts whenever they went out, and about the drastic change in her wardrobe and style of dressing. I told my sister it appeared Dillon came from wealth or hit the lottery. He had the kind of money common folks only dream about *unless* they won the lottery.

I wanted to know what was going on with Sky and this mystery man of hers, if she was she getting caught up in his world of bright lights, glitz, and glamor. I already knew the answer but had to ask the question out loud.

After I finished talking, I thought Phoenix had laid the phone down. When she finally spoke all, she could say was, "Wow!"

I said, "Wow? Is that all you have to say, wow? Weren't you listening? Should I repeat myself? Sky is in a web of some sort. But right now, I really do not know what kind or what to think anymore. I do not want my baby to get hurt, and **wow** is not an acceptable answer, sister dear."

I need your advice as you are the level-headed one that do not get upset and, for sure, do not let things bother you. You have been in school long enough to give sound advice, so please say something other than *wow*!

She laughed and with good reason. She was finishing her degree in criminal justice, not psychology. After her laugher finally stopped, she asked, "When did all this that happen?"

Okay, so she was not really listening as usual, only half hearing. And I started all over again.

She too thought this was strange and said she would ask around if anyone knew Dillon Mason. She promised she would speak to her husband as he was in the entertainment industry, and they both had close friends that often frequent the places that Dillon and Sky visited. Maybe someone would know something.

After hanging up the phone, a thought occurred to me. *What happened to Jasper? His name had not been brought up since Dillon.*

Within two weeks, Phoenix got in touch with me. No one in their immediate circle knew or even heard of Dillon Mason. She said, "Fie, you are not going to like what I am about to say."

She was right—I did not. But I continued to listen as she was good with given advice when needed and sometimes when not warranted like right now.

She told me I was too close to Sky to make a proper and true decision or opinion about Dillon, that I was afraid of losing her to an unknown person that no one knew anything about or even heard of him. I should at least meet the man, get to know him before I make up my mind about his and Sky's relationship. As for the drastic change with Sky, she surmised I was processing too much at one time. Although the change appeared to happen overnight, probably in my mind, only thing it was not in my mind. These changes happen rather quickly in a matter of weeks. And we know, change occurs over time.

Before hanging up the phone, Phoenix said I had a lot of nonissue to work through, and she would help me any way she can. But for now, she told me to get a grip and wait it out to see where it goes. Be happy for your daughter.

I thought to myself, *I can do that. Wait and see where it goes. But for how long should I wait before I say something? I am already not liking what I see taking place.*

Phoenix knew me all too well when it came to Sky—that I did not think clearly and sometimes made rash and or harsh decisions. Maybe she was right. I raised Sky to be an independent person, a person to trust her own instinct and judgment, to examine all sides before making decisions.

In my heart I had this stabbing feeling almost like a dull ache. WHERE IS THE TRUE SKLYAR GRANT?

Where is she now?

What I did know -- she met a man like none of the young men around the neighborhood or in school, a man who was giving her everything she ever wanted and, like most people, saw an opportunity and went for it.

After Phoenix and my conversation was over, I thought, *maybe I am being too judgmental about the whole situation, making quick decisions.* Then I shook my head and said out loud "Shake the devil off."

Each time I saw Sky smiling when she got dressed to go out, I would think, *who would not smile wearing designer clothing and accessories, a limo, and driver at your disposal? Oh well, the Lord will help me sort through all this when it is time.*

Be Anxious for Nothing

Chapter Five

About six months into the relationship, Sky came home one evening and asked me to come outside to see her new automobile.

I said, "Your what? Girl you can't afford car payments on your salary."

She just smiled and kept walking.

Outside was this beautiful black Lincoln Navigator with seats the color of caramel. It was indeed a beauty. I knew she could not afford something like that, let alone the upkeep. As if reading my mind, she said, "Mommie, is this not beautiful? Dillon had it delivered to my job at lunchtime."

So, my question was answered. And I said nothing. I was thinking have you received your dismal papers from you job but thought better not to ask.

She stood there just smiling and admiring her new SUV then said, "Let's go for a ride then out to dinner, and Mommie, wear one of your new outfits I purchased for you."

Once again, I was talking to myself, *this child is telling me what to wear* as I climbed the stairs to go get changed.

When I looked through my closet, I saw new clothes that were not my taste, and Sky knew this. There was shoeboxes, bags with purses in the closet and on the corner of my dresser, a new jewelry box, which I was sure contained jewelry I did not purchase. I would never have brought these things and had no intention of wearing any of it. Although they were uniquely beautiful, they were not my taste or style.

While getting dressed in my own clothing, I felt there was more news to come, but I was not going to ask. I also knew I would have to restrain myself and prepared myself to sit and listen.

When I came downstairs, I noticed Sky had on a new outfit. When she saw me, she said, "Mommie, you are not wearing that, are you? I want to take you to a nice dinner."

I told her what I had on was just fine, and I was not changing.

Reluctantly, we left in her newly acquired SUV. As we drove out of the neighborhood, headed toward the express way, I noticed we were going near the water. Then I saw a sign that read, Malibu.

This was interesting. I see why Sky wanted me to put on a new outfit. These people were elegantly dressed and, personally, I thought, overdressed to be near the water eating at a seafood restaurant.

Once inside, I felt as though everyone was looking at me, and I was sure they were. Compared to the way Sky was dressed, I looked like the hired help, and yet I held my head up as we were escorted to the patio area.

There is greatness and pride in not
caring about what people think
just because they stare at you.

We are all different.

I was always told to be
proud of who I am and
Never hold my head down
No matter what.

Let them stare!

But just for a few seconds, I wanted to run and hide.

There was that feeling again. All through dinner, I was anxiously waiting for Sky to tell me what was going on. When coffee was served, Sky told me she had quit her job and was going to work with Dillon. Not sure I heard her correctly, I asked her to repeat the last part. She said, "I am going to work with Dillon."

So, my hearing was not gone. She did say with him, not for him. I asked, "Exactly what does that mean working with him?"

She ignored that question.

I asked her about school. She informed me Dillon would make sure she stayed in school. At that, I laughed. I asked her if she heard herself talking or if she just memorized all this.

None of the answers given made sense to me nor had I forgotten the question she did not answer.

This child had made up her mind, and at that moment, I was in no mood to argue. I got up from the table and said I would be waiting outside for her to take me home.

She tried talking to me on the way home, and I asked her to stop talking. The ride home was noticeably quiet and strained. I was uncomfortable. For the first time in my life, I did not like being around my own child. It was if I no longer knew who she was or had become.

*Anger locks you into a world
where you can no longer speak.*

The day arrives when I would meet the man who changed Sky

Chapter Six

Several months had gone by before Sky announced Dillon was coming to Thanksgiving dinner, which should be ready around four as they had plans for later that day. She asked me too nicely, *made a few suggestions* of what I should wear to dinner. Now that hit a nerve.

After cooking the previous night and finishing up the day of Thanksgiving, she requested I dress up!

Somewhere in time, she had lost her mind, telling me to be nice, what I should wear in my own house, never mind telling me what time dinner should be ready. Yep, lost her mind or fell and bumped her head. *Hard!*

Standing speechless since we had not talked to each other since the dinner in Malibu, I could have screamed with her demands. I thought to myself, *Oh, my dear Sky, that is not going to happen. But it was nice of you think it is going to happen.*

At last, I finished cooking dinner, which consisted of baked ham, baked hen and dressing, cranberry sauce, turnips and mustards, candied yams, whiskey rolls, potato salad, iced tea, and sweet potato pies.

I asked her to set the dining room table with an extra place setting. To my amazement she did without a word. And I was thankful others would be present when the man himself arrived. As for me, I was more than ready to meet him.

As **I** was getting dressed in my clothes, not theirs, I found myself starting to get nervous as I had no idea what to expect. What I did not want that day was a limo parked out front with security.

At precisely 4:00 p.m., the doorbell rang, and Sky rushed downstairs to answer the door. She had changed clothes and was dressed in a beautiful outfit of blue. I found out later it was tailor made. *(What else was new?)*

In the foyer stood this gorgeous man of six feet three with the most beautiful head of wavy hair, not a strand out of place, beautiful smile and snow-white teeth—the whitest I had ever seen. His navy suit was of exceptionally fine material, not the kind you see in men's shops. There was something different about it. His blue and white plaid shirt had a starch-white collar with four-inch white cuffs held together with cuff links with initials *D.M.*

Upon further inspection, the cuff links held a single blue stone surrounded by diamonds. His shoes were of the same color as his suit. I looked back up at him, and for the first time noticed, he was my age! I kept thinking, *This man is my age!*

I see why Sky was so taken with his good looks. You rarely see men my age that has taken care of themselves to this level. But wait a minute, he was not from our part of town. He was from Beverly Hills. You see men like that on television, and you wonder what they have done to their face. *At least I do.*

I must have stood there staring at him for a full five minutes. I heard Sky say, "Mommie, this is Dillon. Dillon this is my mom, Fiona."

I held out my hand to him, and he did something that caught me off guard. He pulled me to him in a warm embrace and said, "It's nice to finally meet the mother of the woman I love." Upon releasing me, he placed a small box in my hand.

I was speechless but not impressed.

When I was finally out of his embrace, I stepped back and looked from Sky to him, then back at Sky, hoping she was able to tell from my posture or expression on my face I was not pleased with the verbiage "mother of the woman he loved."

One more time, I looked at him then at Sky. I said nothing to either of them about that remark, not even a nod or a smile, just a blank stare at both.

When I looked at Sky, I finally noticed she was dressed in the same color as Dillon, wearing diamonds, and had laid her purse on the hall table. I guess she learned how to complement him by dressing alike.

He was everything she had described him to be, down to his smile, except for one thing—he was my age!

I took a quick look outside, and to my surprise, he was alone. No limo, no security. Instead, I saw a car I did not recognize, midnight blue and beautiful. I learned later from my friend it was a Maserati.

I had a lot of resentment toward this man but knew the time to voice my opinion was not now. Today was a day of discovery, a chance to find out who this man was that had the power to change my child. Or did she willingly go because of his charm and money?

I had forgotten I was holding the gift he had given me in my hand and laid it on the kitchen counter. Once Sky saw the gift, she asked me to open it. I said, "After dinner."

Of course, she asked me a few more times, and I gave her the look that meant stop talking. Finally, there was silence from her as I put the box in the drawer (which I forgot was there—oops).

As Sky escorted him into the living room to meet the family and my friend Marvin, I was left with three thoughts:

1. He is too old for Sky.

2. Who in the world has teeth that white and straight?

3. Who dresses for Thanksgiving dinner in a suit and diamond cuff links?

Dillon definitely was not shy. He acted as though his mere presence demanded attention, and that was just what he got from my family. He was a talker with a hearty laugh. Dillon was the only voice and laughter I heard coming from the living room.

As we all headed to the dining room, he complemented our home, said it reminded him of his nanny's house as it was remarkably like this one. He kept complementing me on the food. Again, his nanny was brought into the conversation. He informed us she cooked food like this all time. He believed it was called soul food and found it delicious. I noticed he was careful not to mention the nanny's name but said several times she raised him.

My mind was racing and in overdrive. Now was the perfect time to ask questions. But because family and guest were present, I thought it best to wait.

Prayer was usually said by my dad before dinner, but Dillon insisted upon blessing the food. When he opened his mouth, the words that came out were surreal. Whatever I had been thinking about him vanished. I was taken in by Dillon, and yet I questioned myself why. What happened during that prayer?

Once the prayer was over, Sky fixed his plate, and he told her how much food was to go on there and exactly where to put it. She looked like she was trained for this. I looked in amazement as everyone else did, especially since the food was placed on the table and to be served buffet style.

As Dillon finished his first serving of food, without him saying a word, I noticed Sky get up and refill his plate. If his water or tea glass was empty, he would point, and it was immediately refilled by Sky.

All through dinner, he was the prefect dinner guest. He talked about his life with his nanny but never mentioned his parents. He told us he grew up in Beverly Hills, travelled abroad regularly, that he personally owned several businesses but failed to mention names or locations. He also said that he owned a few rental houses in the surrounding area but was careful not to mention the city.

When he talked about his schooling, I knew for certain he was my age. If not, he was so close that he would break the numbers apart.

I looked over at Sky then around the table, and all eyes were on him. Everyone was nodding their head except Phoenix. She caught me watching everyone, and we both shook our heads. Even my dad was quiet and listening, and he did not like to sit for long anywhere.

Dillon kept saying, "I have not had this type of food since I was a child living with my nanny." He kept complementing the food until I stopped listening. Last thing I heard him ask was if I cooked or if I had it catered.

Upon hearing that statement, I looked at him and said, "Yes, Dillon, I cooked the entire dinner. We do not have food catered in for the holidays."

Sky saw the look on my face and quickly replied, "My mom is an excellent cook. She doesn't like to, but when she does, she's excellent."

Why in the world does she have to explain anything to him about me?

Before dessert and coffee was served, everyone was leaving as they had other places to stop. I asked Marvin to leave as I wanted to speak with Dillon and Sky in private.

I never spoke to Marvin about Sky or Dillon as we were just starting to get to know one another. And from what I had seen so far from him and the question he asked, Marvin would rather stay and be part of the conversation, and I was not ready for that or need more to think about it as this was just between the three of us.

Once everyone had left, I clean the table and put out dessert and coffee. Sky fixed Dillon a dessert plate but no coffee all the while explaining he only drank coffee from certain coffeehouses after his dinner. That cleared up the mystery of why she did not pour him a cup.

He made a point to tell me he ate breakfast, lunch, and dinner out every day at various four- or five-star restaurants. He did not eat or like fast food, not even snacks.

Since he wanted me to know certain things, I wanted to know what he was not saying. I asked Dillon to tell me about himself, his family, and how he came to be in the Crenshaw area. Instead of answering my questions, he wanted to know if he could call me Mother as he felt part of the family already and how much he loved Sky.

In a calm voice, I replied, "Dillon, you may address me as Fiona or Ms. Grant but not Mother."

If looks could kill, Sky probably would have put me in an early grave. However, she knew not to say a word, correct me, or even look at me.

With my questions unanswered, he grinned at me, stood up, hugged me, and thanked me for a wonderful evening and then he *deliberately* called me Mother. Sky looked at me and smiled. I looked at her, and I am sure I had some type of expression on my face, but it was not a smile. Just like that, they both left.

When she returned several hours later, I was waiting to talk with her. I felt I have been quiet too long and, as her mother, had to say my peace. I knew it would lead to a knockdown drag-out on my part as Sky had turned a deaf ear whenever I brought up Dillon's name.

As she walked past me and did not speak, I demanded that she come, sit down, listen, and not talk till I was finished. Before I could say anything, she started defending Dillon. I guess she did not hear me tell her not to talk.

Because she ignored me, the pent-up anger came front and center, and once again, I informed her, "I would appreciate it if you would not interrupt me while I am talking, and don't run out of the room."

Now that I had her attention, I told her my first concern was the twenty-plus age difference. "This man has lived a full and productive life compared to your twenty-two years."

Sky just sat there staring into space not looking at me. I told her I was concerned about his finances as it was obvious he did not have a nine-to-five job. "Since you are now working *with* him, what exactly are you doing? Where does he get his money? How does he get his money? Are you still in school?"

Sky looked at me with hatred in her eyes. With a voice in nasty undertones, she said, "That is none of your business, Mother."

She slowly rose out of the chair and said, "Are you through talking to me? I have to get packed as I am leaving for a few days with Dillon on a business trip."

I replied, "No, I am not. Please sit down. This is my house, and I am still your mom, not your mother."

There is something wrong about a man having that kind of wealth and cannot or want say how it came to be in possession. When I asked him about his family, he completely ignored the question with a laugh and smile. I cannot recall what he said to you, but I clearly remember the look you gave me. One of those how-could-you looks. I am sure it embarrassed you, and for that, I am *not* sorry. I know you are grown, but you need to wake up.

There was so much more I wanted to say but stopped. I informed her I was done talking for now and that she may leave the room and pack.

Before leaving, she said, "Mother, in the future, you may speak to me in a tone much nicer. If you're not pleased with me or what I am doing, do not speak to me at all." She knew I hated the word *mother*, and she did it on purpose. She also knew me enough to go up the stairs and close the door quickly before I got out of my chair.

I sat there fuming and slowly breathing as I did not want to become ill from dealing with her behavior, especially over a man. I was still trying to figure out when that girl was going to come to her senses and realize the world and environment, she was living in right now was good, but she needed to step back and look at the entire picture, figure out which direction she is going and once she arrived would she be happy. I wanted her to be careful.

I learned over the years that if something comes to you easily or you did not earn it -- you want appreciate what you have until it is gone.

Sky was slowly letting go of everyone she knew from her past, which included Jasper. Jasper was the guy she was dating for four years before Mr. Money Bags with the white teeth, limo driver, and diamond cuff links. This also included letting go of friends she has known for years, some since kindergarten.

I wanted to scream but decided against it. Time was on my side. I know that in order to get through this—whatever *this* is, prayer was needed, and a lot of it. I did not like who she had become, and I was not going to accept it.

Yes, I had a lot of questions about that man, his companies, family, and now Skylar Grant. What exactly did he do for a living? What exactly was Sky doing for a living?

After she left, I needed some me time. I needed to think about the day's event. I took a hot shower, tried to watch television to relax, and it did not work. I sat in the dark and practiced deep breathing as I was really uptight, talking out loud and asking questions that may or may not get answered.

The rest of the night, all I could think about was this older man who was my age, saying he was in love with a woman twenty-plus years younger and how he transformed her into a trophy of his own design.

Problem:

The Trophy Was My Only Child

Emotions Last Ninety Seconds
or So They Say

But It Ain't So

Yes, I Said It Ain't So

Chapter Seven

I would look into her room hoping she would be there, but on so many nights, she never made it home. This made me angry, and yet she was an adult and no longer a child. But the mom in me said, "Maybe, but you are still my baby girl."

One day, I looked in her room. I noticed one of her garment bags lying on the bed and a shopping bag on the floor. I opened the bag. There was a chiffon gown with diamonds and pearls sewed into the neckline forming a *V.* At the bottom of the bag was a black velvet pouch with a strand of pearls and matching earrings. In the shopping bag were shoes and purse to complete her outfit.

The price tags were still attached, so I did the math. The total cost of items made me take a seat on the bed. All these items cost more than I made in a year.

Okay, breathe, Fiona.

Breathe. One, two, three.

Breathe. One, two, three.

Do not give in to those emotions.

Breath. One, two, three.

Do not think.

Just breathe. One, two, three.

Chapter Eight

The next few weeks, I was in total awe.

I had a lot on my mind and discovered that thinking about Dillon took up a lot of my time. I had narrowed all the questions I had down to these: Who are you, Dillon Mason? And what is your end game?

Still thinking about the situation, I realized Dillon could have any woman he wanted. And yet he chose to come downtown. What was wrong with the women of power and stature from uptown where he resided?

Immediately, I felt bad and angry with myself for even thinking that way. Sky appeared to be happy. She was getting everything she wanted and more. I should be happy for her, but it did not seem right. Something felt wrong.

Sky was still living at home but slowly becoming a stranger. I could not talk to her without one of us getting angry, and of course, she would escape to her room, pack a bag, and leave. Each time this happened, days turned into weeks. Up till now, all questions went unanswered. Therefore, I had to take a different approach with her when seeking answers.

The Sky we all knew was gone. Her signature look was gone and replaced by Dillon who insisted she wear more conservative colors and clothing and simple or exquisite jewelry depending on the event. Hair and makeup were done every day. Nails and feet were done weekly so the polish would match her clothes.

After weeks had gone by, I asked Sky if she was comfortable with the change in her appearance. She stared, smiled, and said, "You would not understand, Mother, so I want bother to explain."

But she never answered my question.

I thought to myself, *Oh, Sky, you do not understand. You do not see all that has taken place. You only see what Dillon has allowed you to see. So, my little one, you are* wrong. Now it was my turn to stare at her and smile. Then I walked away—something she was not used too.

I knew it would be a matter of time before Sky moved out. She hardly ever spoke when she came in or would just be leaving with no note, just the sound of the door closing. I had become accustomed to the silent treatment.

A month later, Dillon had his secretary call me to invite Marvin and myself to dinner that week. The day would be my choice. I replied, "I would check my calendar and get back with you shortly."

I immediately called Phoenix and told her what just happened and asked what night she was free as she was going to be my guest for the evening instead of Marvin.

I returned the call, informed whoever answered the phone, my sister and I would be free for dinner this Thursday.

She replied, "A car would pick you up at seven, and dinner would be at eight."

Before I could ask where dinner was going to be, she hung up.

This Too Shall Pass

Chapter Nine

Some time ago, I had a dream about Dillon. In my dream, he was the devil, laughing at me, pointed his finger, and said, "Soon."

Now what the hell did that mean?

Sky came the week of the scheduled dinner with two garment bags and two large shopping bags. Before going upstairs as she had done so many times without speaking, she actually spoke and said, "Hello, Mom," and I almost fell out my chair.

I was in a state of shock that it took me a few minutes to compose myself before saying anything. I did not want a lot of questions flying out my mouth. I was still angry with her and did not want to spoil this dinner or fight with her before I had a chance to meet Dillon again and hear what he had to say, if anything.

I watched as she went up the stairs. I could hear her opening and closing the doors. This went on for about thirty minutes before she came back downstairs where I was sitting, drinking coffee. My heart was beating with joy as she sat down opposite me until she opened her mouth and said, "I brought you a gown to wear to dinner tomorrow night."

My heart sank. I swallowed hard and said, "Thank you."

I really wanted to say, "What is wrong with the clothes I have? It is just dinner." But I thought against it as I did not want to be ignored and have her go into silent mode.

Later that evening, I went upstairs to see what had been chosen for me to wear. Hanging on the closet door was the most beautiful evening gown I had seen as I definitely did not own anything like that. It was a red satin gown with a *V* cut in back with what appeared to be hand sewn rhinestones outlining the *V*. (It appeared Dillon really like the *V* cut style.)

Behind the gown was a red and white satin shawl with pockets. On the floor were shoes. On the bed was a purse with a note on top. The note read, "Look inside." There was a gold chain necklace with a solitaire diamond and matching earrings. I was speechless and almost forgot to breath.

I did not know Sky had been standing in the doorway until she said, "I am glad you like everything. By now I am sure you know or have guessed all Dillon's clothes are custom made, and so are a few of my gowns. While he was having a suit made for dinner, he wanted you to have something special to wear as well, so he called and ordered you this gown with a few alterations from his favorite store."

Instead of "thank you" coming out of my mouth, I just shook my head. Once I heard his name, the dress was no longer beautiful and certainly held no sentimental value to me regardless of what outlandish price everything cost. Sky knew how I felt about Dillon. But she was home, and I did not want to argue about a gown. I was just glad she was home.

Now I was starting to wonder what type of dinner I was attending and why.

I kept having bad feelings that something was not right, that one day the devil would show his true form in the body of Dillon Mason.

I was about to call Phoenix when the phone rang, and a voice said, "Ms. Grant, you have a 2:00 p.m. hair and nail appointment with Sky's hairstylist and manicurist." Before I could reply, she added, "Do not be late and hung up."

Now who made those appointments? I knew the answered as soon as ask the question. Dillon.

Chapter Ten

Did he have everyone on his payroll? Did Sky know I still had a regular job, and taking off for a hair appointment was not in or on my to-do list? Then I laughed to myself and thought, *Oh, Lord, here I go again talking out loud to myself. One of these days, those two will have me laying on a shrink's couch if I do not watch myself.*

Suddenly I remembered I had not called Phoenix to let her know the dinner was going to be formal. While speaking with her I described my outfit in detail and was hoping she could picture everything as I was describing it to her. I told her wear the black chiffon and sequin gown she purchased on her last shopping trip to New York.

At last, it was Thursday.

As I stared in the mirror at myself, I admitted I looked surprisingly good for a lady my age. I wished my James were alive to see me. I whispered, "James, if you can hear me, be with me tonight and keep me safe. When you hear me talking too much, wrap your arms around me so I can feel your presence and know it's time to sit still and be quiet."

The doorbell rang at precisely 7:00 p.m. In the doorway stood Gage. In my opinion a very large and handsome man with a Jamaican accent

He held out his hand as I walked down the steps. I immediately looked right and left to see if my neighbors were looking, and yes, they were all outside. I straightened up and walked with my head up as I knew for once in my life, Fiona Grant was looking fabulous!

Gage escorted me to a white limo and held the back door open. Once Gage had gotten in the driver seat, he informed me he was going to pick up Mrs. Phoenix Anderson. In just that short of time, I had completely forgotten about my sister.

As soon the limo turned the corner, I called Phoenix and said, "You are not going to believe this, so I won't spoil the surprise. We are on our way to your house."

Now I have been in limos before but only the ones taken from the airport to my various job assignments when working out of town. But those limos did not even come close to this one. I could tell right away this was a custom job. I could have lived in this limo for a few days and never miss my bed.

So, this is what Sky was getting accustomed to. I just smiled and put my head back.

I heard a faint noise and noticed Gage had put on soft jazz. The music was coming through very nicely. He let down the partition to inform me Mr. Mason had stocked the bar with champagne, wine, fruit, and cheese for us to enjoy on the way to dinner. The lights were turned off overhead, and soft white lights surrounded the entire back of the limo. That was when I noticed that the carpet was red, which made the white leather seats stand out.

When the car turned the corner, I looked out the smoked windows and saw we were approaching Phoenix's house. And just like my street, a few folks walking had stopped to watch as the white limo stopped in front of my sister's house.

I could not wait to see the expression on Phoenix's face, and she got in I was not disappoint when I saw the look of glee in her eyes. Her face had this ginormous grin. I do not know if it was for the limo, the fact that Gage was holding out his well-manicured hand for her, or his good looks and accent.

She was looking very chic in her black dress and hair pinned up. After she finally stopped grinning, she looked around the limo in awe. I offered her a glass of champagne, wine, fresh fruit, and cheese from the bar. We both laughed, both thinking the same thing: where are we going for dinner?

An hour later, we finally arrived, and the back door opened.

Once out of the limo, we were staring at the most beautiful, magnificent hotel and restaurant we had ever seen. It was utterly amazing. The sheer scenery itself was breathtaking, and as we began to walk to the front entrance, we heard the waves of the ocean.

As we reached the entryway of the restaurant, the doorman opened the door, and it was if we stepped back in time. The foyer was exquisite. While standing in the foyer, we were approached by a gentleman that informed us Mr. Mason and guest was waiting in the dining area. We followed him, of course looking and taking in everything we saw. I was amused by the paintings on the wall. Soon we were in the largest and most breathtaking dining room with a stage that held an orchestra.

I saw Sky coming toward us, and as I reached out to embrace her, in three strides Dillon was there and hugged both Phoenix and myself. I saw Sky step back and said how delighted she was to see us. Not glad but delighted.

To make matters worse and of course I was on edge as she whispered, "Mother, I am so glad you and Auntie are here. Dillon just ordered drinks.

You looked beautiful, Mother, and I am glad you wore the gown. Dillon said he knew that color would look stunning on you. He picked out the accessories. Do you not just love it?"

That was the second time she mentioned Dillon and the gown. Right then and there, I wanted to pull off the dress and all that went with it. *Damn that man!*

I just smiled. I never said a word. I did not think or let my emotion get the better of me that night. I decided to relax, watch, listen, and enjoy the evening. I had noticed it before that Sky on occasion had start calling me Mother—a name she knew I dislike.

Dillon ordered a bottle of Dom for the table, and when it arrived, the maître d' poured. There were no menus handed out as he had taken the liberty to order for everyone.

Phoenix whispered to me, "What if I do not like what he ordered? Speaking directly to the maître d' she said, "I would like to see a menu please?"

The maître d' looked at Dillon, and he nodded his head yes. Phoenix did not order but read everything on the menu. I knew her well. She was looking at the prices.

Sky looked over at Phoenix and said there was really no need to order as Dillon had selected a wonderful dinner selection, dessert, and wine to compliment the dinner. "And Mother, he knows you do not care for seafood, and he ordered you something different. I know you both will enjoy the dinner he has chosen."

But Phoenix kept on reading the menu as though she had not heard a word Sky had spoken.

Thinking to myself, I really wanted to say, "Okay, Sky, how long have you been discussing my likes and dislikes of food with him, and what else have you told him?"

Food started arriving, and they were right—we both enjoyed everything, even the dessert. This was the best-tasting food I had eaten in a long time. I did learn one thing that night, expensive food does not come in large quantity. There are not seconds.

Afterwards, Dillon ordered me coffee while the three of them continued to drink wine. I was sure it was a mistake that the wine menu was left on the table, so I took a peek. The wine they were drinking cost five hundred and fifty dollars a bottle, and they were on the second one. I guess that was why my sister was enjoying it so much.

Phoenix and I excused ourselves to go to the ladies' room. I asked Sky if she would join us and, without taking her eyes off Dillon, replied no.

After four hours of being entertained, it was time for us to leave. We all walked out together. I was excited we would all be riding back together. Then to my surprise, only Phoenix and I got in the limo. Dillon leaned in and said they were staying over in the city for a few days as he had business to attend in the area.

Sky said, "Mother, you really do look divine tonight." She handed me an envelope and said, "Take care. We love you."

As if on cue, Gage drove off.

I looked at Phoenix, and she could see I did not want to talk as I leaned my head back and closed my eyes. There were hot tears slowly coming down as I held the envelope in my hand. I could hear jazz music softly playing in the background. Phoenix called her husband and was telling him about our evening out as I took out the bottle of unopened wine and poured me a large glass.

When we arrived at Phoenix's, Gage open the door for her and waited until she was inside her house, then drove in the direction of my home. Once we arrived, he escorted me to my door, waited till I opened the front door, said good night, turned, and walked away.

Once inside, I realized I still had the envelope in my hand. Sky had written on the envelope, "We love you, Mother." I looked at it for a while and finally placed it in my nightstand along with the others I had been given over a period of time. I was thinking, I *was now* we, *and now I am* Mother *instead of* Mom *or* Mommie.

At that moment, I realized things would never be same. I had to accept it and move on. In my heart, I knew Sky was now living in Dillon's world. Whatever world that may be, it was not the one she was brought up in.

You Can't Focus on the Past.

You Can't Go back and Fix It.

What's Done Is Done!

CHAPTER ELEVEN

I had to get my life back on track and find normalcy and equilibrium. Right now, I had to focus on myself or go crazy worrying about Sky and what was taking place in her life. Whatever it was, I know she was not about to tell me, for she knew I would not approve. At this point, it was in my best interest to keep busy and find the norm that would allow me some inter peace.

A few weeks later, she returned home to pick up a few items. Her hair had been cut with at least twelve inches taken off and styled. Although it looked beautiful, I was shocked as she had never cut her hair, only had it trimmed. She saw the expression on my face and quickly said, "Dillon wanted me to have my hair cut and styled to complement my new wardrobe." He assured her the new look would show off her features and makeup better.

That night, they were going to see a play. After the play she, meaning they, would like for me to join them for dinner afterwards. She would phone the time, and a car would be picking me up.

Now when did this happen that I was no longer given a choice if I wanted to go or not? It sounded like a demand rather than a request. But I went along with it. Now sometimes I would wonder why or maybe it was to be near Sky.

This saddened me greatly that a man can have that kind of control over another person. I did not think she realized how caught up she was in his world. Whenever she spoke, it was Dillon this or Dillon that and *Mother.*

While waiting for her to come downstairs, I was remembering when we would sit and talk for hours, go to the mall, long walks, flea markets, or the movies.

On Fridays, she would be planning her weekend with the girls or going out with Jasper.

Now when she would come home, there were always garment bags and several shopping bags.

This particular evening, she stopped midway the stairs to inform me she had placed a package on my bed, and I was to wear it to dinner. This girl had gotten on my nerves always telling me what to wear as if I did not know how to dress.

As I climbed the stairs anger slowly built up inside. I did not want to become conformational as I wanted to see where all this was leading.

My intuition as a mom never changed. My thoughts were always the same. I was slowly being convinced that Dillon was the devil or at least one of the top-ranking officers.

Sky followed me into my room and said, "Mother, I brought this because I wanted you to look nice to night. We're taking you to the Marina to eat at one of our favorite spots," which translated to his favorite restaurant.

I told her I would go if she promised to stop calling me Mother. She looked at me and said, "It's just a term of endearment."

I was not sure if she heard me, *but* I heard her. I repeated myself, this time with authority in my voice, *"I will go if you stop calling me Mother."*

We stared at each other for what seems like hours, but it was only a few seconds as she knew Mother has had enough of being called mother. Sky knew how far to push me and gave in reluctantly.

She kept her word and called after the play.

I showered and changed into the clothes she or he had purchased, looked into the mirror, and thought, *This is not Fiona Grant.* The outfit was stunning but not for me, not my colors or style. This was Dillon's choice as I had seen Sky in these colors lots of time—black and cream. Sky knew my style in dressing, but I surmised this was all Dillon.

I truly disliked this man until my insides were on fire. I did not know how much longer I would be able to deal with any of this.

I turned my mind from Dillon and started thinking about Sky. I wanted to know how she was spending her days, what was she doing working with Dillon. I know school was no longer a part of her life. Although Dillon had told her she would continue going to school, that turned out to be a lie.

Dillon had changed everything about Sky. Her hair, vintage clothing, even the car she had brought herself, all gone. Her wardrobe now consisted of black, navy, cream, brown, more black, navy, cream and brown. She was too young to wear those colors every day. **I** was too old to wear those colors every day.

Everything she wore now was high end or tailor made, even her jackets, all paid by Dillon, or so I thought. I could not have been more wrong. He had given her a black card of her very own, and he was paying the bill. Up till now, I had never heard of a black card.

Thinking back two years ago, Sky dressed in vibrant and happy colors. She was like my fashion consultant. When I went shopping, I would know what colors were in for the season. Those days were gone. Now on those rare occasions when I would see Sky, her style was very professional. On special occasions, which was about seventy percent of the time, they both had on the same or coordinating colors. He was always smiling, but my Sky was not. She looked sad.

I started thinking I could have been a better mom or maybe I should have done this or that, and just maybe, this would not be taking place. Those were my feelings, and I shared them with no one, not even my closest friend, La 'niece. I started experiencing empty feelings of loneliness because Sky was never home.

I called Phoenix, and we talked into the night like we used to when we were teenagers, only this time, it was me talking and she listened quietly. After about thirty minutes, I asked if she was still there. She replied, "Yes, Fie, I am still here. I am thinking about all we have talked about, done with those two, and how much Sky has changed. You know this is not good. I got a bad feeling. It's not going to end well, and you, sister, should be careful."

We said our good nights, and I thought about her warning to be careful. Be careful of what and of whom? Sky or Dillon? Little did I know that the warning and of whom was wrong. I should have been careful of them both.

To keep from being lonely, against my better judgment, I asked Marvin if he would like to move in with me and give up his apartment. Within the month, he was there

A big mistake on my part but loneliness makes you do irrational things!

Find a place where there's joy and the joy will burn out the pain.

—Joseph Campbell, mythologist, writer, lecturer

Chapter Twelve

A few months later, Sky had gone to the house to get some of her personal things and noticed Marvin's car parked out front. Another car was in the driveway. She had her key, so she walked in. What she witnessed was Marvin and a woman in the den making out like teenagers.

She immediately called me.

I was in total shock, and that was putting it mildly. I immediately left my office and headed home. Not realizing the extent of the shock, I was in, I was sitting in my car not moving. An hour had passed, and I was still in the parking lot in the same spot.

My cell phone rang. It was Sky inquiring where I was. I informed her, "In my car in the parking structure."

She knew I had assigned parking and said they would come get me. Twenty minutes later, I heard a knock on my window and unlocked the door. For the first time in three years, my daughter hugged me and said how sorry she was as we walked to her SUV.

As we approached the house, Sky said in a calm voice, "Mom, it's going to be okay."

Then another voice said, "We're getting you out of that house, Mother."

Only then did I notice Dillon sitting in the back seat. He was smiling with black sunglasses on and looking straight ahead.

When I got home, no one was there. I phoned Phoenix, explained what happened, and within the hour, she was there. She put her arms around me, and only then did I cry.

It seemed I was crying about everything that had taken place. What just happened in my house just made matters worse. It seemed like my life was falling apart and I was going with it. I believe everything happens for a reason. But for now, it was too much to process.

I blamed Marvin for his stupidity. Without questions or answers from him, it was over. There was no coming back from this. We were over. Done.

I wanted to blame Dillon for his part in destroying my life, maybe for all of it. He had come into my perfect uncomplicated life and slowly started taking it apart. It all started that day when he met a beautiful young woman name Skylar Grant on a street corner. But I knew what Marvin had done was not Dillon's fault.

I discussed the idea of moving with Phoenix to get a new start. Then I spoke to Sky that I would be looking for a place to move, putting the house up for rent until I decided what I wanted to do.

She squealed with delight at the thought of moving and wanted us to find a place in Beverly Hills. Without realizing my voice was raised, "Girl, have you lost your mind? Beverly Hills on my salary?"

She assured me that splitting the rent between the two of us, we could do this.

But Beverly Hills, Sky? Really?

Consider it pure joy, my brothers and sisters. Whenever you face trails of many kinds, because you know that the testing of your faith produces perseverance.

—James 1:2-3, KJV

With *everything* that was going on, I honestly believed my faith was being tested.

After thinking about it for a few days, I said to Sky, "Go ahead and see what is affordable."

Within two weeks, Sky had found a place. I agreed to go see it, and to my surprise, it was a beautiful townhouse in Beverly Hills. It had two master bedrooms, a guest room, and two separate balconies. I loved it. Before the smile became permanent on my face, I asked about the rental cost followed immediately by "Have you lost your mind?"

This had to be a joke or a hidden camera somewhere. I could not afford a place like this on my salary. But if I could, this would be it.

Sky said not to worry, it was all taken care of. I had no idea what that meant. She reminded me she would be helping pay rent and expenses. I was waiting for the punch line, and it came a lot quicker than I had anticipated. Before the big move, the *I* turned into *us* and the *us* meant Dillon.

She explained he would be staying there for a day or two every other week as he own several properties in the surrounding area. He would pay her half, and I of course, would pay the other. I was thinking why he could not pay the entire thing. Just as quickly as that thought came in my head, I dismissed it because I did not want to owe him anything.

My feelings toward him had not changed. However, living in the same place would give me a better opportunity to know Dillon Mason.

Within three weeks, I had a Beverly Hills address with underground parking, swimming pool, hot tub, and masseur on the premise. I took two weeks off work, and Sky was there every day. True to her word, Dillon was there for a day or two every other week.

Our new home was more breathtaking each time I entered. I could not wait for Phoenix to come over and enjoy the view and amenities. I was constantly having an awed moment, and when Phoenix came over to see the place, she was pleased.

One day while driving to work, it occurred to me that I might learn to like the man since I did not have to be in his immediate surrounding every day.

This would allow me the opportunity to give him a fair chance. I know my dislike for him helped push Sky to him.

And just as quickly as those thoughts occurred, they went away. I was not going to blame myself for everything that had taken place. I was a good mother, and I knew it. I gave her what I could afford and taught her the difference between want and need.

Dillon came along and gave her both, wants and needs. I did not cry often, but this time, there were tears. I made a promise that I would try to get along with Dillon for Sky. I truly felt if I did not, he would destroy my family even more.

Later that day, I phoned Sky and said, "I wanted to cook something special for the two of you and expect dinner to be at seven." Sky phoned back that Dillon had made reservations for us at eight-thirty that same night. So much for my plans. It seemed that he had overridden my request.

But I had made a promise to try and get along with him, and I was determined to do my best for as long as I could. Wow, this was going to be a challenge as I really did not care for him.

Sky came home and watched me get dressed. After I changed three times, she finally said, "That looks better."

We left by way of limo and was going to meet him at the restaurant.

At dinner, I apologized to them both for my previous behavior and thanked them for getting us such a beautiful place. Dillon assured me it was okay, that I deserved the best, and from then on, I would be treated like royalty while in his presence as I was the mother of the woman I love.

When he said that my stomach knotted up, and a pain went through my chest. I was hoping neither one of them noticed my facial expression.

After hearing those same exact words for the fourth time, mother of the woman I love, I knew something bad was coming and soon.

But that night, I just wanted to enjoy my dinner and keep the peace. I sat quietly and enjoyed the ambiance of the restaurant.

———

Six months living in the townhouse was great. The move was just what I needed. Dillon was true to his word staying with us for a day or two each week. Nine months later, I was told he would be moving in permanently.

My room and patio quickly became my haven.

As it happened around that time, my company had just hired new recruits, and I would be busy arranging their hiring packages, airfares, houses for the next eight weeks, and hiring new trainers. So I would not be home much. Not to mention one of the new recruits caught my eye and held my interest. His name was Casper, tall, chocolate, and bald.

CHAPTER THIRTEEN

Over a period of a few months, I watched Sky being transformed from a happy person to Dillon's servant. I wondered if she realized or noticed the change in her behavior. Dillon would sit there, and she would do whatever it is he wanted done, oftentimes with just a nod of his head.

One evening, I watched Dillon sitting at the kitchen table. Sky was in the living room watching television. He called for her to bring him sparkling water. Now the water was in the kitchen, and all he had to do was get up and get it. Instead, Sky was in there in a matter of seconds, poured water into a wine glass, and handed it to him.

My instinct was stronger than ever. I was seeing and hearing all this, and I knew in my heart something was wrong with this relationship. I was sure of it.

He was slowly taking ownership of the townhouse, which in the beginning was Sky's and mine. He knew I saw the gradual changes in Sky's servitude to him as he would often stare at me as though so say, "Say something." Those eyes I once saw as beautiful now appeared black each time he and I stared at each other. I did not like what was taking place. I could have left at any time, but deep down, I felt Sky needed me.

Sky phoned my job one afternoon and announced the three of us would be going to dinner that night. She pleaded with me to wear the outfit she laid on my bed as this was a very special occasion. As I held the phone in my hand listening to the dial tone, I was thinking, *A special occasion? Now what?*

Before I finished getting dressed, Sky came home alone, which was a shock because they were always together. As I came out of my room, she was right behind me in a beautiful gown. Sky said Dillon had gotten dressed at the spa. We were to meet him at the restaurant.

Gage was outside waiting by the limo. I was praying there would be no security escort. God heard my prayer. There was no escort. We were driven up a steep hill to a restaurant that overlooked the entire city. Regardless to which direction you looked, the city was beautiful as if you were watching a light show—so many colors of lights blinking all at once.

Upon arrival, a valet opened the back door of the limo. I felt like I was home watching the awards except there was no red carpet. By the time we reached the door of the restaurant, Gage was there with the restaurant door open.

Okay, here I go again, red carpet without the carpet. I was in full alert mode.

The hostess approached us and said, "Mr. Mason is at the table and awaiting your arrival."

When she said *table*, I was expecting a table in a room of people, not a separate area with no one there but us. He even had a waiter and waitress standing by just to serve our table.

Siting there in tinted glasses, he did not rise to greet either of us. Instead, our chairs were pulled out and napkins placed in our laps. Dillon did not touch his menu. I watched as Sky ordered for him then for herself. Lucky for me, I got to order what I wanted.

There was small talk made by Dillon. Sky remained quiet and hung on to his every word, never taking her eyes off him. I had no idea what he was talking about or to whom, so I continued to enjoy my dinner and wine.

After dinner, champagne was brought out and poured. I refused the champagne, and wine was poured into my glass. That feeling I had been having crept up again. I held my breath as I could feel his eyes on me. Whatever was going with those two was about to be revealed.

Dillon looked directly at me and asked for Sky's hand in marriage.

I choked on the wine, and when I got my coughing under control, I did not look at him but at Sky. I wanted to see if there was happiness on her face. Instead of her expressing any emotion, she held her head down. I could see her fumbling for something in her handbag.

Sky spoke at last and said they had already set a date. She showed me this white ring box that held her wedding ring—an exceptionally large yellow diamond. Dillon proudly said with a grin on his face, "Mother, it's six carats and very rare."

She pulled out another ring box that held his band. That band had so many diamonds. I laughed as I did not know men wore that many diamonds. Then I remembered this man had money and the means to do whatever he wanted, even wear a cluster of diamonds.

I spoke directly to Dillon, "If the two of you have set a date, why ask me for her hand in marriage?"

He replied, "Because she insisted. She also wants you to design her dress. I explained to her I already had arranged a fitting for her and told the designer what I wanted to see her in. But after countless discussions, I gave in.

"Now, Mother, I know you design the 'working woman's' clothes, but I have never seen your work, especially a wedding gown. Sky assured me you can do it." He made it sound like I did manual labor.

Sky looked at me with no expression on her face and asked if I would design her the perfect gown for the perfect wedding. I replied, "I will do my best."

Dillon placed a card on the table of the designer and stated he wanted the gown to be the way she would have designed it. I never touched the card or looked in his direction. I could feel him starting at me, but I never looked his way. I kept my eyes on Sky. Still no expression on her face. Finally, he raised his glass as did Sky and said, "To us."

My glass never left the table.

The ride home was incredibly quiet as I had nothing to say to either of them the rest of the evening.

Each day is shaped by big and little moments.

—The Ultimate Checklist for Life

Chapter Fourteen

In six weeks, I had designed the gown Sky wanted. Three weeks later, it was completed, and she looked absolutely stunning. This was her day, and the bride's decision should be considered, not his designer's. Not this time, Dillon.

Eight weeks later, we flew to the wedding, which included Sky and our immediate family. No one was there for Dillon, and I asked no question. The vows were exchanged, and just like that, I had devil for a son-in-law. After the wedding, Dillon asked again, "May I call you Mother?"

I replied, "Dillon, you may address me as Fiona."

Only three wedding pictures were taken, one with Dillon and Sky, one with Sky alone, and the last one with Sky and our family. Dillon refused to be in the family picture. Inside, I smiled.

Without me knowing, he had arranged for the designer he originally wanted to design the wedding gown, to make a tea-length gown for Sky to change into right after the wedding. He stared at me and smiled. I had no expression on my face as I was sure he was hoping to see anger there. Instead, I said, "Sky, you look nice."

We walked them to the valet section of the hotel, and there waiting for them was a white Rolls-Royce and Gage. Before getting in the Rolls, Sky handed me an envelope and said, "You and Auntie have fun."

After they drove away, we looked inside to find twenty-one hundred bills. We both laughed and said at the same time, "Guilt money."

A year after the wedding, I had to go away on a business trip for three weeks.

Upon returning to the townhouse, it looked just like it did before we moved in—clean and empty. I did not think a robbery had occurred as the place was too clean. I went and spoke to the manager. He informed me a moving van had showed up a few days ago, the keys were returned by my daughter, and she asked that he give me the security deposit back along with an envelope.

The envelope was in Sky's handwriting. Inside was a note telling me they had moved, that my furniture was in storage, and it had been paid for six months. Also, inside was a check in the amount of five thousand dollars made out to Fiona Grant. No explanation was given. No "Goodbye, Mom." No "I am sorry, Mom." Just the location of the storage and number of the unit, 666.

I drove to Phoenix, and we sat on her front steps. She did not know anything was wrong until I showed her the envelope. She read the note twice and offered me her guest room. All I could think about was that Dillon had come in my home, my life, and taken what was mine, my only child.

Too angry to cry, I prayed for their safety and comfort for myself.

Chapter Fifteen

I took the check and put it with the other unopened envelopes in the storage unit.

I sold my other house with the hope of finding another one soon. Within six months, Phoenix and I found a nice house. With the monies from my other house, I put the entire amount down as I wanted to hurry and pay it off and did not want a huge mortgage.

Next on my list was to clean out storage unit 666. I took my time and separated my clothes and furniture I purchased. I was leaving everything Dillon and Sky brought behind in one of the brown boxes or on the floor. That included clothes, shoes, purses, jewelry, and the few pieces of furniture they brought. I did not care what the storage owner would do with it, I just didn't care. I wanted no reminders of Beverly Hills and especially of Dillon Mason. However, I made sure I took all the unopened envelopes.

Once I was all moved in my new house, I took a month off work to learn the area and enjoy my patio.

I phoned Sky, left a message to say that I had sold the house, and purchased another in another county. I gave her my address, told her I would be keeping the same cell number, and hoped to hear from her soon. I did not bother to tell her about all the items I left in the storage unit.

Every day I was hoping she would call. I started calling once a week, then once a month, and finally after six months, I stopped calling, praying one day she would reach out to me.

My heart was telling me Sky was gone with Dillon somewhere to some unknown maybe remote location. But I knew my girl, and one day she would be back. So I waited. I had lost my child to the devil, but being a true believer, having faith in God, I knew the devil could not keep what was not his.

Reminiscing back to 2000, when I started to feel things and see signs that something was not right, I should have spoken up.

On that Thanksgiving dinner, seeing him for the first time and speaking with him, I knew something was amiss about this man. But who would have believed me if I spoke my mind? I talked to my sister about these feelings of guilt, and she would say, "Girl, it's just you being overly concerned about your only child. Sky is a smart girl and knows right from wrong."

Well, that may be true. But a mother knows what she knows. Sky was in pain.

A year had passed, and I had started receiving calls, but no one would be there on the other line. I knew it was her. Every other week, the same thing. I would say, "Sky, it's okay. I am here if you need me."

Six months later, she did call and spoke. I had to force myself to breathe, to just listen. She never told me where they were living, only, "Mom, I am all right" and would hang up before I had a chance to say anything. I could tell from her voice she was lying. She also knew if she stayed on the phone, I would probably ask questions. I did not want her to withdraw, not call again, or hang up.

I stayed quiet. Then a thought occurred to me. She was with Dillon and allowed her to call but was listening.

My heart ached because I missed her so much. And yet I had to be very patient or risk losing contact with again.

Chapter Sixteen

Two months later, while I was sitting in my house, the phone rang, and when I picked up and said hello, the other person had hung up. I knew it was her again. Was she trying to tell me something?

May of the f next year, my door rang. When I opened the door, there stood Sky. I quickly opened the screen door and opened my arms for her, and she came to me willingly for only a brief moment. I hated to let her go. Then I looked behind her and understood why she stepped away so quickly. Her husband was there, still grinning and wearing dark sunglasses.

Dillon pushed Sky aside as though he was my child. He reached out to grab me, but I stepped away and asked them to come in. I looked outside, and there was no limo, just an ordinary car. I did not ask questions. I did not offer any refreshments. I wanted to listen, and yes, I had more questions than ever, but felt I needed to hear what they had to say.

Sky said, "We just dropped by to see your place."

And to this day I had never forgotten the words that came from Dillon. "Mother, is this what is called the ghetto?"

I was shocked. But I could not ignore that remark. I replied, "No, this is my home, and it's not the ghetto." *And this time, I shall not be moved.*

A few months after that visit, they both appeared at my office. Right behind Dillon was a florist carrying an enormous bouquet of flowers. With that big grin of his, he said, "These are for you, Mother."

I asked the florist to place the flowers on the corner cabinet. Because I was at work with my door open, I whispered, "Do not call me Mother. My name is Fiona."

They wanted to take me to lunch, and since I had not eaten, I accepted.

Once outside, I was looking for the limo, Sky's SUV, or his fancy car. Instead, there was a Hummer parked, and knowing Dillon, I knew it was theirs.

I was right. Sky informed me this was hers and that she no longer had the Lincoln. I asked her what happened to the limo, Gage, and the other automobiles. Both were quiet. Neither one replied.

What happened next left me with my mouth open. Sky opened the back door for Dillon to get in and closed it after he was seated. I opened my door, climbed into the front seat, and my mind went to a dark place, but I said nothing as Sky got into the driver's seat. I looked back at Dillon. He had on dark glasses and was smiling.

We got to the restaurant; the valet opened all doors. Dillon still had on his glasses and now had an even bigger grin on his face. Sky ordered his food then hers. I, of course, ordered for myself.

All the while, my mind went to that dark place, which was like an empty hole.

After the table was cleared and I was waiting on my coffee, I looked directly at Sky and asked if she was all right.

She looked at Dillon, and he responded, "Yes, she is fine, Mother. Probably a little tired from all the driving."

I spoke to him as calmly as I could as we were in public, "Dillon, I was asking Sky a question, and I would appreciate it if you let her speak for herself. And if she is tired from all the driving, why you do not drive?"

He looked at me, smiled, raised his hand for the check, and Sky paid the bill.

I was being dismissed or ignored, and I dared to venture which one. Being quiet was over for me. As we waited for the car to arrive, I asked my questions and if he wanted to answer questions then here goes, "What happened to make you move from Beverly Hills? Why did you think if was okay to put my personal effects in storage? What on earth were you thinking to leave me a note and a check with the landlord? Where did you two go for almost five years with no communication of any kind?" And the big question, "Why are you here now?"

Of course, none of the questions were answered. It was as if I was talking to myself, and that made me angry, so angry I could feel the fire rising through me and I felt I needed a timeout.

On the ride back to my office, Sky never said a word. It was like she had lost her voice. I now knew for sure something was wrong.

Back at my office, neither got out. I grabbed Sky's hand and kissed it. Dillon just sat in the back seat, wearing his dark glasses, smiling, looking straight ahead. I hated to see them leave, but knew I would see them again.

I gave the flowers to my secretary.

*   *   *

Still angry when I got home, I was sitting on the patio having a glass of wine. I called Casper and invited him over for wine and a lite dinner. Within the hour, we were both enjoying a second bottle. And for some reason, I thought of the unopened envelopes I had placed in a box upstairs in my closet.

I went to retrieve the box, returned to the patio, and placed the box on the table. I removed the top and placed all the envelopes on the table in front of Casper and explained these envelopes contained guilt, shame, and love tokens.

As I opened each envelope, there were cash and checks. The checks that were no longer valid, I put aside to be shredded. Casper did the honors of counting the money as I called it out. Over the years, there was a total of fifty thousand dollars in cash and checks.

We each had another glass of wine, placed the monies and checks back in the box, and I decided it was time to make a deposit. Casper agreed.

CHAPTER SEVENTEEN

A year later, around nine at night, Sky appeared at my house in tears. First thing I looked for were bruises. Satisfied there were none, I led her to the living room and sat on the sofa. I told her to talk to me and tell me what was wrong. She laid her head in my lap and cried for almost half an hour. When she finally stopped, she said, "Mom, it's all gone. We lost it all. You were right. The cars, limo, and plane were leases. The offices he maintained were what is called virtual office. All gone.

"Dillon is broke, Mom. The house we were living in was leased. The owner sold it, and we must move within thirty days. We have no place to go." Sky looked at me, I was sure, for answers and or a solution to their problem.

I had four questions: "Why were you living in a leased house when he claims to have rental properties? What do you mean he lost it all, and how? What about his many business he talked about? More importantly, how could a man such as Dillon Mason lose everything?"

Honestly, I found this hard to believe, but it could be possible. And yet I found myself smiling.

Sky started to repeat herself as though I did not hear her the first time. I did. It was Sky who was not listening to my questions and, of course, offered no answers. After some time had passed and she finished telling me what she wanted me to know, I asked, "Where is Dillon now, and why did he not come with you?"

"Mom, he had me park two streets over and walk here."

I looked at her and said, "You have got to be joking! He had you, his wife, walk here in the dark, at nine at night while he sits probably in the back seat?"

Without a smile on her face, she said, "Yes, Mom."

Her next statements almost caused me a heart attack. She asked if they could move in with me for about six months, maybe less until Dillon could straighten all this out. He said it was all a big misunderstanding.

"Sky, what happened to your common sense?"

My mind went into recall mode of the beautiful townhouse we shared in Beverly Hills, how the two of them moved out with no warning or regard for me. Although they paid for six months of storage, the sheer thought of even putting my belongings in storage was enough to make me angry all over again, the letter to the manager, note to me with a check in it, and silence from Sky for *five long years*!

I did not allow myself to respond to Sky right away as I was angry at them both, for her being stupid and him just because he was the spawn of the devil and took my child from me. He sent her because he knew I would not say no. *Well played, Dillon.*

I took this time to make a fresh pot of coffee and poured a cup just for me. Sky had this surprised look on her face as if I should have given her an answer right away. I said nothing, drank my coffee, and looked at her. Finally, I asked, "Why did not Dillon come with you and ask me himself if his intention is to stay here?"

She replied, "He knows you do not like him."

I responded, "I do not, but he is your husband. Go get him so we can all three have a civil conversation."

Once they returned, I asked, "Dillon if you lost everything, what do you plan to do, and how are you going to take care of your wife?"

He responded, "I still have money put away here and there and can obtain other resources if needed."

After that statement, I did not want to know what any of that meant. Looking at them both, I said, "For six months, you can move in, but your furniture will have to go in storage, and not my garage. Month seven, if you are a man of your word, you *will* be gone."

He looked at me and smiled. I felt a chill, a cold chill. The devil was moving into my house.

I would come home from work; he would be sitting watching television. Sky had begun waiting on him, driving him wherever he wanted to go as he sat in the back seat with those dark glasses on. They were living in my house but never received mail. It was like they did not exist.

Sky and I no longer had mother-daughter talks as he was always within earshot, always listening, always answering if I asked her a question.

My questions to him were always the same: what really happened to all your wealth and business? I never got answers, just that grin I had come to hate. I sometimes wonder if he did own anything.

I saw Dillon as the devil wearing a smile that covered up the ugliness in his heart. I would always believe that once he had lost everything, he formulated a plan. He knew I would do anything for Sky, so he manipulated her into getting what he wanted, including my money.

It was Sky who always came to me when money was needed. She went from, "Can I borrow five hundred, Mom" to "Can I borrow one, two, or five thousand dollars," each time with a promise to pay it back. I had no problem lending her the money as it was their money, they had been putting in envelopes for me over nine years. So it did not matter that it was never paid back.

When their money plus the interest that had accumulated ran out, then it became a problem. Whenever Sky asked for loan, I wanted to know why but never got an answer. This time, they needed to borrow ten thousand dollars.

Having said no for the first time, I felt guilty and wrote out a check. But before I handed it over, I asked Sky and Dillon what they did with all the money I loaned them. With that grin of his, he replied, "I am making business transactions to get us out of here."

I was not satisfied with the answer he gave and said so. He walked away with Sky right behind him. They went upstairs without my check, which was the last of my personal savings.

I wanted a better answer than what he offered as I knew it was a lie. He never left the house. And when he did, it was to the gym or spa. Sky did not go anywhere but to the store and back. Other than that, he was always in "his" chair, watching television.

After that I was treated as though I was a stranger in my own home. I never saw them when I came home but heard him reading his Bible. I can only imagine her sitting their obediently. I did not like who she had become and blamed Dillon.

A few weeks had gone by, and they both started coming downstairs, always together. Sky would start talking to me, and he would sit in the same chair in front of the television wearing a grin, dressed in a suit without a tie, but he would have on his diamond cuff links. Sky dressed in the same color as he did but now they had nowhere to be.

Dillon approached me as I was drinking coffee on the patio one evening and asked again to borrow ten thousand dollars, and of course the same old question issued out from me, "Why?"

I did not wait for an answer. Instead, I said, "You've been at my house well over a year, and it's time for you to go. So yes, I will loan you the money. Maybe it will help your business ventures speed up the process of whatever you're trying to accomplish and of course move you out."

Without looking at him I went in the kitchen, got my purse, and pulled out my checkbook. I wrote the check and laid it on the table. I could feel his cold eyes on me as he picked up the check and walked back upstairs. No "thank you," no nothing.

Chapter Eighteen

One evening when I returned from work, Dillon suggested we all go to dinner. Sky was not in an evening gown but looked just as elegant. Dillon always dressed nice even when sitting in front of the television. And much to my surprise, I was not asked to change clothes.

The routine of going somewhere was always the same. Sky would open the back door for Dillon, and of course he would be wearing dark glasses and smiling.

At the restaurant we dined at that evening, everyone knew him. The valet was given twenty dollars for parking the Hummer. The doorman was given ten dollars. The hostess was given twenty dollars just for seating us. The manager came out personally to meet him and said, "Mr. Mason, so nice to see you again."

A hundred-dollar bill was placed in his hand. Dillon sat at the head of the table and the maître d' ask if he wanted the usual. He said, "Yes, and bring a bottle of sparkling water and a plain glass of water with ice for my mother-in-law."

Once he returned with the water, he was given ten dollars.

Dinner was brought out. So was a bottle of wine. This person was given twenty dollars. I thought this was excessive but said nothing. After Dillon tasted his wine, he looked at Sky, nodded his head, and she drank hers. After dinner was over, he left a fifty-dollar tip on the table.

The Hummer was brought around, more money was given out, and he of course got in the back seat, still with the glasses on and looking straight ahead, telling Sky where to go for his coffee and dessert. Sky felt the need to tell me Dillon never had coffee and desert where he ate.

I replied, "I remembered."

I was starting to believe she had been brainwashed or she was terrible afraid of him. One thing for sure, she had replaced Gage as his chauffer.

I started paying more attention to what was going on when I was with them. There were so many signs something was not right, only I could not figure it out. What I did know for sure was that Sky was no longer happy, and it had nothing to do with everything being gone. No, it was more than that. Her total behavior and demeanor had changed.

Dillon's behavior had become so erratic that it started to worry me. He would read the Bible daily, not that anything was wrong with it, but I had never seen him pick up a Bible before. He started teaching Sky the Bible, and when I heard him preaching in the house, I thought he had gone mad. He asked me on several occasions to join them in taking Communion. I always refused. Next, he was wearing a clergy collar around his neck, always riding in the back seat with dark glasses, now wearing a clergyman's collar and a Bible next to him.

Six months turned into six years, and they were still here.

Dillon was still preaching in the house, takin Communion upstirs in the bedroom, going to the gym and spa daily with Sky being the chauffer.

No one was working in the house but me. And looking at him made me want to vomit and shake some sense in to Sky.

She did buy food for the house and prepared his food as if in a restaurant. He would sit at the table with a cloth napkin, place setting, serving wares, and two glasses, one for water and the other for wine. One day out of curiosity, I asked Sky, "Why is there only one place setting when there is three of us?"

Her response was, "Dillon prefers to dine alone."

Now after dinner he had coffee at home, upstairs where Sky took it to him on a tray.

She took her meals with me, which made me happy as we were alone. As soon as I started talking, we could hear him coming down the stairs. I believe he thought I was going to ask Sky about his business. What he did not know was that I no longer cared about him or his affairs. But poor Sky would not say anything, not even nod her head. So she ate in silence, always with me talking.

One Saturday while Dillon was upstairs taking a nap, I asked Sky if she was enjoying the gym and spa. She said, "Mom, I sit in the car and wait for Dillon."

For the second time, I saw her crying. Without looking at me, she said," Mom, I am afraid and do not know what to do."

My baby was hurting. Something was terribly wrong. I knew what she had just told me took a lot of courage. One day—and I prayed soon—she would tell me everything.

One morning while in the kitchen preparing to go to the office, Dillon came into the kitchen and said, "Mother, I am so happy we're here."

My response was, "How much longer do you plan to be happy here? When are you going to get a job?"

What he said next, I could feel anger coming through me. With that devilish grin of his, he said, "I sent Sky out this morning to look for a job as I have the Word to spread among the people. That is my true calling, Mother. I am a man of God."

I stood there staring at him for the longest time, saying nothing. I just stood there as though time had frozen.

When I did trust myself to speak, I said very calmly, "Dillon, you are not a man of God but the devil in human form. What kind of man sends his wife out to look for a job while you sit all day doing nothing? You are power hungry and very controlling. You have no friends, so just who are you spreading the Word to, Dillon?"

He said nothing. Not one word. He just started laughing as though I said something funny. As quickly as he started laughing, he stopped and grinned at me, turned, and went to "his" chair and turned on the television.

Chapter Nineteen

Another year had gone by with only Sky and I going to work.

*   *   *

For Christmas, Dillon gave each of us a mink coat. *Now where did the money come from?* Sky was incredibly happy with her new coat. It was the third one he had given her since they met. My coat remained in the box on the floor. He left the room and returned wearing a full-length fur coat the same color as Sky's.

Before I left the room I, could not hold my tongue any longer. I asked Dillon where he got the money to buy three fur coats. I knew the job Sky had was not enough to pay for even one. I was not expecting an answer, but he did reply. His response was, "Mother, just be happy and enjoy your gift."

I kept walking but with a cold chill, my coat still in the box on the floor.

Later that same evening, Sky had made reservation for a restaurant in Beverly Hills, and they both were dressed in the same colors and had their new coats in hanger bags. I wore one of my own coats and paid no attention to either of them when they suggested I wear my fur. That fur was still on the floor where I left it that morning.

Before reaching the restaurant, she stopped, and they put on their furs. I shook my head and looked straight ahead. At the restaurant, there was a line of people waiting to get in, but as usual, there was no problem with the Mason family getting in. His door was opened first; money exchanged hands. He was greeted at the door; money exchanged hands. Their mink coats and my coat were taken, and money exchanged hands. I overheard the hostess say, "Mr. Mason, your table is ready for you and your party."

Sky ordered for him. He said nothing the entire evening and never took off those dark glasses.

Once back home, I asked Dillon if he was hiding from someone. I caught a brief glimpse of Sky shaking her head, and the expression was one of fear.

Dillon smiled and said, "Mother, it's none of your business. Sky, it is time for us to retire for the evening."

I spoke directly to Dillon and said, "As long as you live in my house, everything you do, Dillon Mason, is my business. I do not know what's going on and am not sure I want to know, but if it involves my house or Sky, I have a right to ask and know."

He turned and smiled at me. Held out his hand to Sky and said, "Come."

She looked back at me and mouthed *I love you, Mom.*

My face became warm, and I did not realize those were tears rolling down my face.

A week later, Dillon approached me, smiled, then hugged me from behind. I could feel the negative energy flowing from him. He said, "Mother, you've made me so happy that we are all together. You are the family I never had. Sky and I are going to give you at least six grandchildren. Would that make you happy?"

I looked at him as though seeing him for the first time. *Does he really think children will make me like him or solve their problem? Does he not hear or remember what was said last night?*

Instead of answering his question, I asked, "Where is Sky?"

I had not seen her since last night.

He said, "She's not well and is resting."

I wanted to see for myself. As I headed to the stairs, he blocked my way and said in a loud voice, "She is resting and doesn't want to be disturbed!"

And hour later, Sky came into the kitchen and said she had not been feeling well. I asked her, "Did your not feeling well have anything to do with the conversation Dillon and I had last night?"

She never answered.

As she was leaving the kitchen, without turning around, I said, "If he is hurting you, call 911. But if you can call me, I'll be there a lot quicker."

She went quietly back upstairs. I turned around to see her nod her head and wipe her face. I heard a second pair of footsteps go upstairs and knew he had been listening. *Good, Dillon. I hope your heard me well.*

A Storm Is Coming

Chapter Twenty

Sometime later, the next day, they both came into the dining room, Dillon with that devilish grin and the coldest that followed, Sky standing by him. She said how happy they both were to be here with me. Dillon said, "It feels like old times when we lived in Beverly Hills."

Okay, he is certifiable crazy. The good times in Beverly Hills lasted only for a short time. Then I was left behind, but who knew maybe he was speaking of his good times in Beverly Hills when he had lots and lots of money?

I looked at them both and said, "What are referring to? You both left without a goodbye, moved my things into storage, and left me a check. Is that Dillon, what you are referring to about the old times?"

Dillon started laughing and walked away with Sky right behind him.

A short time later, Dillon came back downstairs and found me sitting on the patio reading a book. He took the book from my hand and stared at me. His eyes appeared black, and again I felt a chill. It seemed like each time he came around me I was always cold. I did not like being looked down on or at a disadvantage, so I stood up to stare back at him. Before he could speak, I told him in a calm voice, "Dillon, you are interrupting my quiet time. Please hand me back my book."

He just continued to stare at me all the while holding my book. I was not going to be defeated by this man, so we just stared at each other. Eventually he placed the book on the table and turn to leave. With his foot in the door,

I said, "Dillon, I do not know who or what you are, but I am not Sky and not afraid of you."

He turned to look at me and said in that voice I heard some time ago, *"You should be, Fiona."*

As I sat there thinking about what just happened, my cell phone rang, and I jumped. I quickly answered, and it was Casper. I told him to come over and have coffee so we could talk.

When he arrived, I made us lunch and we talked. After lunch, I was telling him the things that had been taking place and the changes going on with Sky and Dillon. He just looked at me in disbelief. He assured me it was all in my mind. That there was no such thing as the devil living in my house.

When he left, I remembered this verse from the Bible: "It is God who arms me with strength and makes my way perfect" (Psalm 18:32, NKJV).

For some strange reason, I knew I would need *his* protection.

Chapter Twenty-One

Another six months had gone by, they were still here, and everything appeared to be normal, only it was not normal.

* * *

Sky and I decided to go play bingo.

As we were leaving bingo that night, she called Dillon to inquire if he wanted food or coffee as we would be stopping before coming home. He did not want anything, not even coffee. Dillon refusing coffee was strange, but she thought nothing of it.

As we pulled into the garage, the lights were on, and the back door that led into the house was unlocked. When we entered the house, I felt that chill again. My intuition told me something was wrong. I felt strange. A weird feeling came over me. I became restless, and I mentioned all of this to Sky. She laughed and said, "Oh, Mom. You and those premonitions."

As she proceeded upstairs, I gave her a big hug and said good night. She looked back at me and said, "Good night, Mom. I had fun tonight."

I went to my room, and for the first time since they moved in, I left the door open. I lay on the bed with my clothes on, including my shoes, still having all these strange feelings and now feeling restless.

Almost within minutes, I heard Dillon raising his voice, calling Sky everything but Sky in a very strange voice, one I was not used to hearing, and yet I knew it was him. Upon hearing Dillon go on and on and Sky being quiet, I was getting worried but did not leave my room. Instead, I sat up on the side of the bed.

Then I heard her say, "Stop! You're hurting me!"

Then there was quiet.

Still in my room, I listened again, and it was quiet.

Minutes later, I heard Sky say, "You should leave, Dillon, or I'll call the police."

I heard Dillon say, "I am sorry. I did not mean to hurt you. Let us pray."

I was thinking to myself, *they are having a disagreement. He has caused pain, and he wants to pray?*

About two hours had passed, and he started yelling again, this time calling her whore being born of a bitch. He kept saying, "You and all your friends are whores. Any woman who goes out alone with her mother as you say to play bingo, which I do not believe, should die and go to hell.

Now you expect me to believe you and your girlfriends are planning a four-day trip? Sky, you have no girlfriends. I saw to that personally. Did you ever wonder why they never came around? Money can buy anything especially when offered enough. Did you ever wonder why I had you drop out of school? I, Dillon Mason, made you who you are, not your precious bitch of a mother. And yet you are still ignorant. Or do you think I am stupid? No respectful woman leaves her husband to go anywhere alone with her mother and especially not with girlfriends."

Sky asked him, "Why can't a woman go somewhere without her husband? What is wrong with it, Dillon?"

His response shocked me. He said, "It's the law. My law!"

Suddenly, I heard this strange voice again, saying, "I know you and mother did not go play bingo. I know you were with another man or out there looking for one. I think we need to have a baby right now. I do not want to wait any longer."

Sky said, "NO! No kids! Not now! Not ever! Not with you, Dillon. You're evil and mean. Now leave me alone."

Dillon replied, "I knew you were a whore. I would not want you to have my child. You are not worthy to have my child. You are just like all the rest of the women out there, unclean—including your precious mother."

I had heard enough of the kind of talk. I got off my bed and headed toward the front of house. I went to the stairs and called Dillon and got no response. "Dillon, I know you hear me! All right you be quiet and listen. That is probably better. But listen good as you know I do not like to repeat myself.

"I've had enough of your loud talking and being disrespectful in my house. It is one thing for you and Sky to disagree. But when you started using that type of language and calling your wife a whore and the audacity to call me something other than my name? Well, mister, you have gone a little too far!

"I do not like getting in whatever you two are arguing about as I do not know what it's about, nor do I want to know. Just keep your hands off each other before it goes too far.

"And, Dillon, remember this today and going forward: this is my house, and that's my law. If you do not like my law, you can always leave. Just you, Dillon, and do not leave a forwarding address. Sky stays here."

After returning to my room, my bones became cold, and I found myself sweating. I had a feeling of uneasiness that something more was coming, something very, *very* bad.

Dillon had started his own private war with Sky and me, his sworn enemies. Now I knew the devil was truly in my house—upstairs in the bedroom.

It became quiet upstairs. I did something I never did and that is *to assume.* Therefore, by assuming it was over, I allowed myself to sleep.

*Time Allows You to See
a Person for Who*

They Really Are

CHAPTER TWENTY-TWO

I was awakened by a faint scream, "Momm . . . mie!" So I sat up in bed and heard it again, "Momm . . . mie."

I ran up the stairs and stopped, stopped in disbelief at what I was seeing.

I could not believe that my child was lying on the floor with her head bobbing up and down. Not realizing I was looking at blood, I kept thinking why is all that *that black stuff coming from Sky's mouth?*

I must have stood there for a minute or two, but it seemed like hours had passed as I watch Dillon with his foot in her back continue to strike her in the head. With tremendous blows, her head would come up off the floor and then back down.

I thought I was dreaming and realized this was no dream! Dillon was killing my child!

I screamed at him to stop hitting her, to get off her, and leave my house. He slowly turned around with those black eyes, looked at me, and said, "Oh, so where am I supposed to go?"

I replied, "I do not care, but you have to get out now, or I am calling the police."

Dillon took his foot off Sky and kicked her so hard in her side until she curled up like a fetus and moaned, "Oh God. Mom, help me . . ."

He started off down the hallway, laughing.

As I was kneeling to check Sky, I did not see Dillon when he turned around in the hall and headed back into the bedroom. Before I knew what was happening, he grabbed me from behind and threw me behind Sky, which caused me to break the mirrored closet door.

I remember I bounced from the shattered glass of the closet and hit my head on the edge of the nightstand. I could hear Sky quietly saying," Stop! Do not hurt my mom!"

I did not realize the blood that was on me was my blood from the gash on my forehead. The pain I felt in my head was unbearable. Dillon came toward me again, this time with his fist. All I could do was put up my arm to ward off the blows, but they just kept coming. I heard something crack and could not move my arm. It felt so heavy. I could taste blood and no longer see out of my left eye. I felt helpless and could barely move. There were no tears. Just pain.

I heard a muffled sound, "You are killing my mom."

The sound of Sky voice gave me enough strength to inch my way to her and gently nudge her with my foot. I said, "Baby if you can stand up, run. Do not look back and get help. I am okay. I will find you."

Sky could barely stand up. She fell twice. Dillon took advantage of this and once again kicked her hard in the side, causing more pain. She stopped moving but somehow managed to make it downstairs.

I stood up holding my side. My arm felt as if I was carrying something heavy. I said in a clear but loud voice, "STOP! Leave her alone, Dillon. You want to hit a woman, come hit me."

And to my surprise, those black eyes headed back up the stairs and, with his fist, hit me in the face. I fell backward.

Moaning and crying softly, I managed to see Sky roll down the second flight of stairs. When I heard her hit the mirror, I knew it would not be long before she was out the front door open. I could hear Sky screaming, "Help us! Help us please! Call the police!"

Then there was quiet. There was no screaming from Sky. She was safe. I knew the police would be there soon. I tried to smile but was in so much pain. I silently prayed as I heard Dillon laughing. Neither of us knew if the police were on the way, and what happened next still gives cold chills.

I was still lying on the floor. He came to me, straddled me so tight that I could feel his ankles pressing my sides, and started punching me in the face and head with his fists. Then he stopped and walked away.

I heard moaning and realized it was me still by the door of the bedroom, too sore to move. I did not know when the hitting stopped or where Dillon went. But I knew I had to get up and get out the house.

Struggling to stand up, and finally I did, I started heading toward the bedroom door. That is when I saw Dillon coming around the bed with a ceramic lamp, wrapping the cord around the base. I was thinking, *what is he doing? The bulb is still in there.*

He started hitting me with the base of the lamp until I sank to the floor. Again, he straddled my body so I could not move. The pain was so unbearable until I felt nothing but the blows and felt blood flowing.

He continued hitting me, saying, "I am not going anywhere." He kept hitting me till the base of the lamp shattered. I prayed the hitting was over until I felt something sharp digging into the top of my head. I realized it was the part of the lamp that held in the light bulb. The bulb was broken, and this mad man was digging the silver part of the bulb into the top of my head.

I was trying to get away from him, but he grabbed my shirt, and I heard it rip apart from the back. My back was exposed; he stepped on me as if I was not a person. And maybe in his distorted mind, I was not. He was the devil, and that night, anyone that got in his way was going to be hurt. I was still on my back and in so much pain that it was hard to move and breathe. He grabbed my head, bent down, and said, "Mother, can you hear me?" I just moaned, and then he hit me again.

Finally, it was quiet in the bedroom. I could hear Dillon down the hallway laughing.

I managed to crawl down the stairs to the first landing and thought I was safe from Dillon. I looked in the mirror and saw him at the top of the stairs holding a vase. I crawled down the last two steps just in time to watch the vase shatter the mirror and see pieces of glass falling on to the floor.

In only seconds, he reached the bottom level and started stomping me in the back. Then I heard a crack. I heard the front door open and felt myself being dragged out. I felt the cold concrete as my head was pushed down then a few sharp kicks in the side.

More laugher.

The pain had left my body numb. There were no tears. I did not know if I was alive or dead.

I was waiting for a hit, kick, something. When nothing came, I managed to get up on one knee but not for long. I fell face down. After several falls, I lay there on the cold concrete. I pushed myself up, and the pain was back with a vengeance. I tried again and again to get up but each time fell, each time worse than the other.

When I finally managed to get up, I could not stand up straight but was bent over. For the first time, I cried for myself. Silently I prayed, "Lord, help me find my child in the darkness and the quiet." Then I fell down again, this time on my knees. I heard laughter and just knew it was from Dillon. But as I listened, it was coming from a distance.

I looked to the left and right and saw people looking but no one was moving. I noticed four men standing, drinking, pointing, and laughing my way. As the laughter continued, I prayed Dillon was gone.

After three or four tries of trying to get up again, I moved toward the school area. Somehow, I knew that is the direction Sky would have chosen.

*   *   *

That night was like a movie in slow motion and main characters was Dillon Mason as the devil, Skylar and Fiona Grant as the victims.

*   *   *

I remember being tired and noticing the streetlights were on. I saw folks on the sidewalk looking and not moving.

I could feel blood running down my face. And because of the laugher I heard, it must have been funny seeing a woman limping and falling on the sidewalk screaming, "Has anyone seen my daughter? Has anyone seen my daughter? Which way did she go?"

More laughter.

Dogs barking.

Chapter Twenty-Three

I could make out two figures standing in a driveway and did not know if I was imagining things because of the severe blows to my head or if I was really seeing someone. As I got closer to the two figures standing under the streetlight, my mind was racing, and my heart was beating so fast. But I kept walking toward them and discovered they were both men. They just stood there, hands to their side. One of the men held up his hand and said, "Stop!"

Instead of stopping, I kept limping forward and said, "I am looking for my child. Have you seen my daughter?"

It never occurred to me they did not know my daughter. Both looked at me and shook their head. One of them spoke, "No, we have not seen anyone tonight, just you."

My knees gave way, and I fell flat on my face. One of the men reached down and helped me up, took off his shirt, and put it around me.

I looked down at myself. Blood was now coming from various parts of my body. I notice I had on a bra, jeans badly stained with blood, and no shoes.

The laughter I previously heard had stopped.

Someone shouted, "That man has a gun! Call the police!"

I felt myself being dragged, pushed toward and behind large trash bins at another house. The man who had given me his shirt looked down at me and whispered, "Sshhh. Stay behind the trash can, and do not come out until we come for you or the police."

All the while he was talking to me, I was thinking, *where is Sky? I have got to find her and get her to the hospital.* Then I remembered someone had shouted that that man had a gun.

I heard that crazy laugher and knew it was Dillon. I was thinking, *where and when did he get a gun?*

Lots of shots were fired. More shots were fired followed by laughter. Then there was another shot. Then there was another shot. It seemed the shooting went on forever. I could hear people screaming, dogs barking. I could hear glass shattering as the bullets hit windows. Whenever a car or car window was hit, alarms went off.

There were so many shots fired, and I became afraid Dillon would find me and finish the job he tried earlier, and that was to kill me. I was praying whoever lived in the house would come out and offer me safety. Instead, I saw the lights go out. And I understood. No one was coming. No one but Dillon to find me and Sky.

Dillon kept shooting, laughing, and calling Sky and me. Police sirens were getting closer. But the shooting continued as though Dillon did not hear the sirens. I recognized the voice as one of the men who was standing there previously said, "Hey, man, you shot my brother."

I closed my eyes and starting humming gospel songs to myself. More shots were fired and more laughter from Dillon. He asked where the young woman and the old one went?

Dogs barked. The shooting started again, broken glass and car alarms. More shots.

People screaming.

Dillon laughed and called Sky and me.

More shots.

Dogs barking.

The sound of police sirens and blue lights were on the street. A helicopter hovered overhead with search lights.

The shooting stopped. Dillon must have seen the bright lights from the helicopter. I heard from somewhere, "This is the police! Drop your weapon!"

When all got quiet. Only the barking of the dogs could be heard. I crawled from behind the trash can and could see the back of Dillon running toward the house. I saw him point a gun to the ground and another was across his shoulder. The street was now lined with police cars. People were standing on their lawns.

There was a shot from the corner house, my house. Dillon was shooting at the police. They were shooting back. This lasted for what seemed like hours, but in real time, it was only a few minutes. I started to cry and pushed myself back down to the ground, no longer hidden behind the trash cans that belonged to the people who turned the lights out.

I prayed for my daughter wherever she was and that she be safe and alive through all this.

*   *   *

I was awakened by smelling salt and realized in the back of an ambulance. I saw an EMT sitting next to me, taking my vital signs and calling out info to another one sitting across from me writing on a clipboard. Before they could finish, I wanted to know if anyone has found my daughter, Skylar. They just kept talking and reading out numbers as though I had not said a word. I screamed, *"HAVE YOU FOUND MY DAUGHTER?"*

The EMTs looked at each other, and I knew something was wrong. Although I was severely injured, I knew I needed to be treated, but at the same time, I needed to get away from them to go look for Sky. A police officer came to talk with me, asking questions I was not ready to answer. I just wanted to know if Sky was found and if she was okay.

It appeared everyone had an agenda or protocol to follow. I did not. I just wanted to know about my daughter. Nothing else at that moment mattered, especially Dillon Mason whom I heard was held up in my house. I heard that SWAT was on the way.

No one was listening to me when I asked about Sky. They refused to answer or just ignored the crazy half-naked woman bleeding. I thought, *that's okay, folks. I will go find Sky myself. The street is not big.*

Not thinking of my own injuries, misjudging the height of the ambulance, and forgetting the pain I was feeling, I removed the oxygen from my face, got up from the cot, pushed past the EMT who was saying something that did not have the phrases "young lady," "her daughter," or *Sky* in the sentence.

By the time I reached the back door of the ambulance and stepped down, I fell to the ground **hard**. I was helped me an EMT to sit on the back step of the ambulance, and this time, I was given something for the pain. I was warned not to move as I was going to be transported to the hospital as soon as the police officer asked me a few questions.

From a distance I heard, "We have a young woman savagely beaten! Send the paramedics to this location now!"

I knew they had found her, and I started crying. Sky had been found and would be receiving medical treatment.

I could not see when they brought her out from wherever she had been because policemen were standing in front of me. They stepped aside, and that was when I saw her strapped to a gurney. She was unconscious. The EMTs were speaking very rapidly, "Her pulse is very weak! We are losing her!"

"No pulse!"

"Paddles! Stand back!"

I watched as they shocked her, and it seemed like she jumped up in midair and back down. The monitor was still the same with a slow beeping sound.

Again, I heard, "Paddles! Stand back! We got a faint pulse! LET'S MOVE!"

I saw the blue line I had seen so much on television and again heard slow beeping sounds. I knew this was not good. What I heard next made me scream. "SHE'S CODING! WE HAVE GOT TO MOVE NOW!"

I watched as they drove away with Sky, and I wanted Dillon dead. I was supposed to have been in the next ambulance. But I was not going anywhere. My child was dying or possibly dead. And Dillon was going to pay.

I no longer felt pain. I had no more tears. I felt nothing. My heart was racing, and killing Dillon was on my mind. He would die or I would.

The Storm Came

and

It Was Mother

Chapter Twenty-Four

I saw several people that had been shot being driven away in ambulance. As each one passed, I prayed for them silently. The two good Samaritans that helped me had been shot, and each one was in an ambulance.

I had no more tears or fear. My body should have been sore, but I felt nothing. I willed myself to move away from the ambulance to ignore the pain that racked my entire body and to stand up and do what I must do for Sky, to show Dillon Mason a real *mother*.

I had started to bleed again. The EMT that was talking said, "You needed to go to the hospital and be treated."

I refused to go. I knew my rights and could not be forced to take treatment of any kind. I signed the release liability form. I saw a policeman go over to the last ambulance on the street as they were pulling away. He said something, and they stayed parked.

A policeman walked over and informed me that the gunman was held up in my house, and it was not safe for me to be there. He pointed to the ambulance at the corner, saying that that one was for me. But I knew what needed to be done, and I was not afraid to do it.

He looked at me, and I was smiling. He asked if I was okay. I said, "I am fine. My child was in that first ambulance and had to be shocked back to life twice, and then it may or may not have worked. The man that shot up the street and wounded people is held up in my house. And you ask if I am okay? Yes, officer, I am fine. How about you? You okay? You still waiting on SWAT to get a strategy together before they break down my door?"

He looked at me and replied, "Ma'am, we'll soon have the man in custody."

The two scenario that played in mind were the following:

1. Dillon would be taken into custody. He would turn on the charm, hire a lawyer, and be free.
2. He would die tonight.

I do not remember walking toward my house or speaking to anyone after that. I had one mission, and that was to get back into my house and face Dillon.

I kept hearing the word *code*. I was more determined than ever to face the devil himself. Oh **yeah**, I was going back into **my** house.

There was so much chaos happening all at once. Gunshot victims, helicopters overhead, news vans parking all everywhere, policeman during crowd control not to mention car alarms still going off. No one paid any attention to me as I headed back toward my house. I kept thinking this is easy. But every few steps I took I was falling causing more pain to my already sore body. But I had to keep going. After the third time of falling, a voice in my head said, *stand up, Fiona. Keep moving toward the house. You got this.*

At last, I was at the front door. As I put my hand on the doorknob, I heard a police yelling, "Stop her! She cannot go in there! The suspect has a gun!"

Now I was laughing hysterically. They called him a suspect. I called him the devil. *And my child had coded!*

Yeah though I walk the valley of shadows of death, I will fear no evil; for thou art with me; thy rod and thy staff comfort me.

—Psalm 23:4

For I am the Lord your God who takes hold of your right hand and says to you, "Do not fear; I will help you."

—Isaiah 41:13

Chapter Twenty-Five

I could hear him upstairs moving around, so I called his name. He answered as though nothing had happened and said, "Yes, Mother."

Holding on to the banister and climbing the stairs, I kept thinking, *I should feel more pain. I am bleeding. My hands are swollen. My head, back, and feet hurts.*

Before reaching that last step, I was met with a big foot that kicked me hard enough that I fell backward down the stairs, bumping into what was left of the mirror at the foot of the stairs and rolled down the last two steps. Before I knew what was happening, Dillon was kicking me everywhere, including my face. I was so disoriented that I did not have time to think or at least shield my face.

Suddenly, he stopped and was saying something that I could not understand. I took advantage of that time and stood up to face him. I only had one good eye but saw him clearly, and I heard laughter. I realized the laughter was coming from me.

I felt his fist hit me in the face. I heard a crack and spit out blood. As he prepared to hit me again, I managed to dodge the blow. I remember my brothers saying, "Hit down low." And that is what I did. I put all the strength I had left and hit him hard enough to knock him down.

He stayed there, holding himself, and it was my turn to kick. And kick was what I did. Down low. Then I started laughing again. I just kept hitting and kicking all the while screaming, "You killed my baby!"

I started laughing again as it was, he who was shielding himself from my kicks. Finally, I stopped and was thinking, *I need a cup of coffee.*

I believe I was hysterical, *or* was I?

I walked away from Dillon as he was holding himself, then I saw him feeling his face. He started laughing that sinister laugh.

I stopped, went back over to him, stood over him as he had done to me, and when he moved, I brought my foot down on that beautiful face of his as hard as I could.

He said, "Bitch, you broke my nose."

I never said a word but walked away toward the kitchen, looking for something to hurt or kill Dillon with.

My pain had turned to pure rage. Yes, Mother had turned into a real mother of a beast. Dillon had no idea of the love I had for my child. I would have swam a river of snot if that was what it would take to protect her. *So bring it on, Dillon. Mother is ready.*

There was so much blood running down my face and out my mouth. My eye had swollen some time ago and was completely closed. I did not care I wanted to kill this man. *My house. My rules.*

I heard pounding at the door and heard, "THIS IS THE POLICE! OPEN UP!"

Ignoring the knocking at the door, Dillon grabbed me from behind and tossed me onto the dining table, so that I fell on the table and then to the floor. In two giant strides, he was hitting me again, and this time, I was not shielding myself against the blows. I was fighting back for all I was worth, seeing my child in the ambulance and being shocked.

I was so mad, spitting out blood and probably a few back teeth. I said, "You hit like a girl," and I started laughing.

He hit me again, and I kept laughing. This time it was he who looked at me and said in a calm voice, "Mother, I am going to pray for you and ask God to forgive you."

"To forgive me? You take your Bible and pray for your own soul."

All the while I was saying this, he had the telephone cord behind his back and suddenly around my neck. I felt him pulling it tighter and tighter and saying, "Die! Die like your precious daughter, and you two can be together!"

Then he laughed that awful laugh of his.

I know now what Psalms 121 (NIV) means: "I lift up my eyes to the hills—where does my help come from? My help comes from the Lord."

I had strength to hit him harder than ever until he released the cord from around my neck. I told Dillon, "I am not dying tonight by your hands."

I was fighting for Sky and myself with everything I had in me.

Chapter Twenty-Six

I did not hear the door as it crashed. Both Dillon and I saw SWAT at the same time. Then I heard, "Freeze!"

He ran upstairs, and I heard the door slam shut. I just lay there too tired to move. I looked up, and there were policemen, guns, and men in black gear that read *SWAT.*

A policeman grabbed me, pulled me outside where another grabbed me and wrapped a blanket around my shoulders. Then EMTs examined me again. Before the door to the ambulance closed, I saw this strange little robot going into the house.

I heard the siren of the ambulance and knew this time they had taken me to the hospital. I could feel what they were doing and hear what they were saying. It seemed like they had done this before. One of the EMTs was saying they needed to stop the bleeding and start calling out numbers again. I felt the sting of a needle. The last thing I remembered was Dillon was still alive.

*   *   *

I remembered waking up in a room with a doctor, nurses, and police officers. I was on oxygen and hooked up to an IV. I kept looking around the room and noticed that in the corner Phoenix was crying. I surmised

I was not dreaming or dead. I kept checking my surroundings and could not speak because of a tube down my throat.

The doctor noticed I was awake and requested that the tube be removed. The man sitting in a chair next to my bed said he was the detective assigned to my case and had a few questions for me. He asked if I knew what happened tonight. I shook my head up and down. He said that before leaving my home, they found my purse and wallet. The wallet contained my emergency contact, so they called my sister.

He explained that pictures had been taken of me when I arrived at emergency care for his report. I asked to see them and felt my body go numb. That was not me. No way!

I had questions of my own like, "How long have I been here? Where is my daughter? Is she alive?"

The doctor, as though reading my mind, informed me I had been in emergency care for six hours. My daughter was taken to a trauma center because of her injuries. He did not know the prognosis of her condition, only that they were severe.

As I began removing the cover, the doctor said, "Ms. Grant, you are in no shape to be discharged, and we still have a few more test to run."

He proceeded to give me details of what they had done while I was in the emergency care unit. They had to release the blood that had formed in my eye by cutting it as my left eye was swollen completely shut. They removed pieces of glass from my head by shaving the top of my head. They removed glass and concrete that was embedded in my face, forehead, and then stitched my face and forehead. He also said I would have bruises for a few days. An MRI was taken of my entire body to detect if there were fractions or broken bones.

Sadly, he said, "You have minimal damage to your brain, left arm and wrist are broken, two broken ribs, fractured chest, and your knee is busted."

If they told all this to Phoenix, and I was sure they did, that is why she was crying.

I was listening and understood all that was being said, but I wanted out of their as I had to find Sky. I thanked the doctor and asked, "When can I be released?"

The doctor looked at me and wanted to know if I fully understood what he had just said. I assured him I did and would have all those treated, fixed, or repaired when I found my daughter and knew that she was alive.

Not realizing how sedated I was, I attempted to get out of bed and hit the floor hard, rolling over in pain. I could feel the IV as it tore through my skin.

The nurse helped me back into bed and said, "The meds should wear off in another hour."

I looked at the nurse and the detective now standing in the corner and said, "I do not have an hour. I need to be with my daughter. NOW!"

I felt a prick in my arm and saw the nurse as he walked away, then blackness.

Chapter Twenty-Seven

When I woke up, Phoenix was sitting by the bed. That same detective was sitting in the corner on his cell and writing on a pad. When he noticed I was awake, he brought his chair over to the other side of the bed. He informed me that upon entering my home, they found Mr. Mason in one of the bedrooms upstairs. He was sitting in a chair near the window, and unfortunately, he had killed himself.

I asked, "How and with what?"

He said, "Mr. Mason shot himself with a semi-automatic weapon, which caused half his head to be blown away."

The body was still in the room where it happened, and as soon as I was able, I would need to go back to the house and make a positive identification before the body can be removed. He asked, "Ms. Grant, do you think you'll be able to make a positive ID?"

I was smiling as the devil was dead and killed himself. *Wow!*

After everything I just heard I still wanted to see my daughter. If Dillon was dead, there was no need to hurry and identify the body.

The detective continued talking about Dillon. He informed me during their investigating of my home that, in addition to finding the weapon next to the body, there was a half box of bullets. In my attic, they found four more weapons with the serial numbers removed, four full boxes of Teflon-coated bullets, several passports with his picture but different last names in a briefcase and an exceptionally large sum of cash. All which had been taken to the police station and marked as evidence. He then asked, "Ms. Grant, did you know about any of this?"

I replied, "No" and looked over at Phoenix in disbelief, thinking how could all this have happened under my roof without me not knowing?

I did not shed a tear for Dillon. I was thinking of the attic. I had forgotten I had an attic because in the eighteen years I had been there, I never used it. The devil found the attic and used it for storage or destruction. He was going to kill both of us, change his identity, and disappear.

A few minutes later, I said, "I want to go see my daughter. If Dillon is dead, he is not going anywhere. NOW SOMEONE TAKE ME TO MY DAUGHTER!"

Now that I had everyone's attention, the doctor said, "Ms. Grant, I am sorry we can't release you in the condition you're in."

I assured the doctor I won't hold them accountable should something happen to me. "I will sign whatever papers needed for my release, but I am going and legally, you cannot stop me."

In case no one believe that I was leaving, I pulled out the IV without knowing what I was doing, and blood gushed all over. I removed the heart monitor, and the machine went off. I was in pain but kept doing what was needed. I remembered the fall, so I asked Phoenix to help me down.

I was in hospital scrubs and socks given to patients. When I reached the door, the nurses brought a wheelchair and papers for me to sign. Ignoring the wheelchair, I took the papers. I looked at my hands, and they were so swollen, I could not sign my name, so I put an *X* for my signature and had Phoenix witnessed.

As we were leaving the hospital, the doctor explained again about the medication as if I did not hear him the first time. I knew the risk I was taking, and because of the meds given, my body was weak, and I was very tired. But it was time to go and see my daughter.

Phoenix car was in the emergency parking lot, and she asked me to stand by the wall while she got the car. As Phoenix was helping me into her car, the detective caught up with us and informed me that the police that was stationed outside my room would escort us to where Sky was taken and that he would be over later to take our statements. I thanked him, and we followed the police car.

Just knowing Sky was in some trauma center in the city, which they were careful not to say which, I was so grateful for the detective that I found myself crying and thanking God for hearing me.

On the ride to the trauma center, my pain had become unbearable, but I was determined more than ever to see my daughter, so I said nothing to Phoenix, not even a moan. I just wanted to keep moving.

I knew if she was taken to a trauma center the injuries, she sustained were bad. I would not let myself think of the worst.

Chapter Twenty-Eight

It seemed like hours had passed since we left emergency care. Although we had a police escort and did not have to stop at traffic lights or Stop signs, it seemed like the distance between hospitals was too long.

Finally, we made it to the trauma center. Once we arrived, there was a nurse outside with a wheelchair for me, so I guess the doctor or police had phone ahead to let them know we were coming. Still in pain, I accepted the wheelchair and was taken to the floor where Sky was being treated.

Once we arrived on the floor, there seemed to be a lot of policemen standing outside her room. A lot of activity was going on in her room, everyone moving amazingly fast and not talking. The only talking I heard was from the actual room itself.

A doctor came and asked if I was related to the young lady that was brought in tonight.

I replied, "Yes. I am her mother."

She asked me to wait outside the room and asked a nurse to bring a chair and bottles of water.

I had so many questions but knew I would have to wait a few more minutes. She went to speak to the police officer and the other doctor that were now standing in the doorway.

Three doctors and a chaplain approached Phoenix and me. Phoenix grabbed my hand and, in a whisper, asked me not to think the worse.

Too late. I had buried a husband a few years back and knew that seeing a chaplain in any situation was bad news. I did not notice the police officer with them until I heard her asking questions. "May I have your name? Who are you to the lady in the room? What is the address? And how did you know the deceased?"

I answered all questions asked but one: "How did I know the deceased?" Because I did not answer, the officer said, she would come back later.

I asked, "Could I please go and be with my daughter?"

Everyone stepped aside as I pushed myself out of the wheelchair, holding my side, and proceeded walking into her room with my sister and the chaplain following close behind. Upon entering the room, I saw the curtains were drawn around the bed, and I could hear voices talking about "this patient."

When I moved the curtain, neither I nor Phoenix was prepared for what we saw. There was Sky lying in bed unconscious, or so I thought, with the right side of her face showing. The left side was bandaged up. I asked the doctor to remove the bandages so I could see my baby's face. What I saw made me scream until I felt a needle prick in my arm and then blackness.

When I woke up, it seemed as though I had been dreaming until I realized I was in a hospital and Sky was in the next bed lying perfectly still. Phoenix was crying again.

The doctor came in and explained, "When your daughter arrived, she was barely alive. She had coded twice in the ambulance and once in the trauma center. Because of the severity of the injuries she sustained, we induced her into a coma." He assured me in time they would bring her out of the coma.

As I lay their weeping, feeling completely numb, he explained, "The left side of her face will have to be reconstructed as all the bones had been broken along with her nose. Her eye had been dislocated and sunk into her head, and she has a punctured lung."

The tube I saw was draining blood that had built up inside and around her lungs. They were concerned about her back as they believed she might have a spinal injury. Therefore, they placed her in a full body brace.

The tube in her mouth was helping her to breath. She continued to explain they needed to insert two IV bags, one in each of her arm. Her neck and back was in a body brace. Now they would have to wait and see.

Hot tears were running down my face. She explained in great detail what would be taking place over the next few weeks to repair the damage and that full recovery time would be at least two years.

I could hear talking as though in a whisper. The clock on the wall was the loudest I had ever heard. So I focused on that to drown out all she was telling me about Sky.

Tick tock. Tick tock. Tick tock.

I looked around, and the chaplain was speaking to me about her faith, then darkness.

I woke and looked to my right, and there was no Sky. Phoenix had called my dad, Casper, La' niece (her godmother), and Melanie (her go-to person since she was ten). I should have been happy to not be in the room alone, but I remembered why I was there unfortunately not how I ended up in the bed. So my question was, where in the hell was Sky?

A nurse was trying to change my bandages, and I could not remember ever getting or having bandages put on except for my eye. Now my arm was in a cast. So what was she doing?

I asked about Sky, and the nurse replied, "She had been taken down to x-ray and will be back shortly."

I attempted to get out of bed, and she insisted she bring in a wheelchair.

Before Sky returned to the room, I requested if they could remove the other bed and bring four chairs. I looked at the nurse, smiled, and said, "I am here for the duration even if it meant sitting in this wheelchair." I was praying that my pain would ease up soon.

Once the bed was removed, everyone took a chair and decided they would wait a while at least till Sky returned from having x-rays. While waiting, the memory of what happened and why we were both there just made me angry all over again. Dillon tried to kill us.

I heard a whisper say, "It could have been worse. You could have been shot in the garage where you might not have been found until he had gotten away."

I nodded my head as if in agreement and thanked the Lord for watching over us.

Another set of doctors came in later to examine Sky but said nothing to me. They didn't look at me and I thought how strange but said nothing.

A nurse came into the room with what seemed like a small novel in a red folder for me to read and sign. I read it and signed all the papers except one, the one about taking Sky off life support should it be needed. After reading it I returned the folder to her.

Minutes later she was back with another folder from emergency care for me. I read it but signed nothing. I knew my injuries as they were already explained to me in detail in the emergency ward at the other hospital. But my injuries would have to wait. Sky was the priority now. I returned the folder to her with none of the paperwork signed.

Chapter Twenty-Nine

That evening, around eight, that same detective that was at the hospital with me came to the trauma center. He said, "I am sorry, Ms. Grant, for what you and your daughter had been through, but there is still the matter of making a positive ID of the man who killed himself upstairs in the bedroom of your house. The quicker you make the ID, the sooner you will be able to return to your daughter."

Phoenix and the other ladies said they would stay at the hospital with Sky while I went with the detective. Casper volunteered to go with me. As we were getting in the back of the police car, I was thinking what a nightmare it was and yet it had only been two days since this all happened.

When we turned the corner on my street, you would have thought a funeral was taking place or had taken place on my street and folks were there for the repast.

Police cars, news crews, cameras, lined the streets, and yellow tape blocked the sidewalk and across the entrance of what was once my front door. My entire front yard was taped off. The door was boarded up with wood as were the front windows. Some nice nasty person wrote murder house in black paint on my garage door.

As we got out of the police car, a microphone was pushed in my face. I never looked up to see who it was, nor did I speak. I remember the detective saying before we left the hospital, "There is a blanket on the seat. You might want to use it."

Now I understood why the blanket was there as Casper grabbed it to put over my head, which forced me to look down at the sidewalk.

There were two policemen doing crowd control so we could get to the front door. The detective instructed us to keep walking. Casper had his arms around me, guiding me to the front door. I never noticed the coroner out there until Casper whisper it to me. I never turned around as I did not care. I just wanted this to be over and get back to the trauma center.

When I got into the house and went upstairs, I looked down at the street and saw so many people standing around looking, watching, or sitting in lawn chairs. It was like a circus, and all that was missing was someone selling popcorn. As I was looking at the people, I saw a few familiar faces and wanted to scream, "Where were you when all this was going on?"

When I stepped away from the window for the first time, I noticed all the blood on the hardwood floor, carpet, and walls. I saw the broken mirrors and more blood. Upon closer inspection, I noticed blood on the banister and the mirror at the bottom of the stairs gone. *I did not notice this when I first got in the house? I guess you see only what you want.*

Looking into the bedroom where I first saw Sky lying on the floor, I had tears started down my face. There was so much blood. My face became hot as I could picture Dillon beating her in the head. I kept looking into the room and saw the closet mirrors shattered to pieces and then the broken lamp. Self-consciously, I touched the top of my head and pulled my hand away quickly as though it was on fire.

Walking down the hallway, I saw more blood on the carpet, cabinets, and walls. Then I saw the bedroom at the end of hall with the door closed and a police officer standing in front of it. When we approached the door, the officer opened the door. The detective went in first then Casper. I did not want to go, but Casper held out his hand and said, "It's all right. He can't hurt you anymore."

My legs would not move. I just stood there. Finally, I took hold of his hand and went in with my eye closed—thanks to Dillon, that was all I had for now. Slowly I opened my eye, gasped, and held my chest.

There was a person in the corner of room with the word coroner on the back of the jacket. There was a body in the corner near the window sitting upright in a chair covered up. Someone said, "Ready?"

I said, "Yes."

The cover was removed, and I just stared. I could not move or talk just stare.

The detective, looking at me directly, said, "Ms. Grant, would you like some water?"

I shook my head no. Then in a stern professional voice, he said, "Ms. Grant, can you identify the body in this bedroom?"

"Yes, that's Dillon Mason."

He asked how I could be sure considering half the face was gone. I looked directly at him and, in a calm voice, said, "The half I can see has a mark on his face that I put there during the struggle, the brass knuckles used to beat Sky and myself, and by the sneakers he had on."

The stomping-and-kicking-Fiona sneskers. That was Dillon for sure. The devil was dead.

After the identification was made, Dillon was removed from the house. I asked the detective if I could stay for a few more minutes to observe the damage that had taken place. Each room had been completed destroyed. My entire house looked like it belonged to someone that was moving out instead of living there. I learned from the detective the destruction I was seeing was done by the police as this was now a crime scene.

Chapter Thirty

Once back to the trauma center, Phoenix started calling our immediate family, telling them what had taken place within the last forty-eight hours. Eventually everyone showed and was in disbelief of what Dillon had done.

Day 4

Sky being in the hospital and in an induced coma, I called Jasper and some of her long-forgotten friends. Since Jasper lived so far away, he was the last to arrive but stayed the entire time with me at the hospital. Her friends had come and left but promised to return soon.

I left instructions along with a list of names at the nurses' station that only the people I listed were to go into her room.

Day 5

Another doctor and the same chaplain came into the room. Seeing them again together, I did not like it but was prepared this time. I had prayed for Sky as I had never done before. The doctor approached and asked, "Is there anyone you want to call? Now would be the time."

Jasper and I stood up together, I looked at the doctor and the chaplain. In a calm voice, I said, "I've already called on my Heavenly Father."

The chaplain smiled and nodded. As they both walked away, I kept saying, "Not yet, she is still here and alive."

Everyone that was in the waiting room started crying as they heard what the doctor had said. No tears from me. I just kept saying, "Not yet. Not yet."

I left Sky room and went to the chapel. While Jasper was sitting with Sky, I would visit the chapel and sit for hours. This time, my dad came in and sat next to me, assuring me not to worry. "She is in God's hands. She is strong, and you have enough faith for both of you."

My child was not going to die.

A doctor and nurse came into the room and reminded me of my injuries. But I would not let them treat me. I was starting to feel pain again, but as long as Sky was in a coma, I could endure the pain. The pain I felt would have to wait until the doctor or doctors came up with a plan of treatment for my child.

Day 9

The doctor came with good news. Still in an induced coma, Sky's vital signs had improved significantly, and they could go ahead and talk about surgeries that she would need. I smiled and looked up and whispered, "Thank you, Abba."

Later that day, a plastic surgeon was brought in to discuss her case and explained what would be taking place over the next few weeks. I gave the only picture I had and said, "Make her look like this again."

He looked at me and said, "I will do by best."

Day 10

An ophthalmologist came and said it was a possibility they could save her eye.

Day 13

The plastic surgeon came in and informed me they were going to insert titanium plates under the skin to reconstruct her face and to keep her eye in place. Also, they were going to repair her nose. I was informed it would be best if all the surgeries were performed while she was in a coma and let the healing start before bringing her out as the pain would be significant.

By this time, I told Phoenix to take Dad home and, if she was coming back, to stop and buy me some more clothes. I was not leaving the hospital without Sky. Since Jasper came straight from the airport to the hospital, he had his suitcase with him.

After they left, only Jasper and I remained at the trauma center. Together we both prayed and waited. I was in so much pain that I could no longer feel anything but knew eventually I would have to be treated and soon.

Day 14

The tube from her chest was removed. The next surgery would be to graft skin from her thigh to cover the hole where the tube was inserted into her side.

Day 20

The doctor had completed all the surgeries, and in five days, they would bring her out of coma. She would be heavily sedated and would hardly feel pain.

Day 26

She moaned. Jasper immediately went to get a nurse and a doctor. While the doctor was examining her, she opened her eye as half her face was still covered by bandages. The doctor reported she looked fine, but he would run some tests just to be sure.

Sky continued to look around the room. She did not know where she was or what had happened. Because of the breathing tube down her throat, she was unable to speak. We were told it would have to remain there until her breathing became normal. Both Jasper and I were crying and laughing. She was awake and alive. Jasper whispered to me, "Moms, her breath smells minty."

I looked at him and smiled.

That evening, I went to wash up in the restroom, and for the first time, I looked in a mirror at myself. I knew why the hospital staff was worried. I felt comfortable with Jasper to stay with Sky, so I had Phoenix take me to the emergency room at the hospital where my doctor was. But that is another story for another time.

My Sky was awake! She was alive!

Now the hard part—telling her about Dillon. I called everyone and let them know Sky was awake but not ready to receive visitors or phone calls. Phoenix, Casper, La 'Niece, and Melanie came anyway.

Day 28

The tube had been removed from her throat. The detective came back and wanted to speak with Sky. We stepped in the hallway, and I informed him the doctor suggested we wait until a psychiatrist was present before talking about her husband's demise. I was also thinking what her reaction would be when I told her I had him cremated.

*   *   *

In the presence of the doctor, psychiatrist, nurse, and Jasper, I told her about Dillon and how he took his own life. She just looked at me then at each person in the room then back at me. I saw the tears and reached out to her. To my surprise, she slapped my hand away and started screaming, "Get out! Get out!"

No one left the room. I was more in shock than anyone was. Sky had to be sedated, and finally, sleep came.

The psychiatrist came back later that afternoon and spoke with Sky and asked if she understood what was said earlier. Sky whispered, "Yes."

The psychiatrist left but not before saying she would need therapy to help her get past that dramatic experience.

Later that evening, Sky asked why Dillon killed himself.

I replied, "He was a coward and took the easy way out."

Her response did not surprise me, "No. You're wrong. He was not a coward. He loved me." Where is his body?

I told her I had taken care of it and have the death certificates she should keep. I did not tell her that I had his body cremate and requested they put his ashes in the large green leaf bag I provided. Took the bag to cemetery and left it on the sidewalk. Nope no need to tell her that. But one day she will ask.

She cried and screamed at me and it was ok. She was alive and to be honest I was not listening to what she was saying. The nurse wanted to give her a sedative and I said no, and I knew she was going to get the doctor. I also knew it would take few minutes before they return with a sedative, I had to show tough love. I looked long and hard at Sky and asked, "Do you know what happened to you, to me? Do you know why you are in the hospital, and I look like this?" Your husband almost succeeded in killing you. I handed her my compact mirror so she could see herself.

She said nothing but cried. I wanted to comfort her but thought against it. I explained to her what all had taken place at the house, the surgeries she had, the number of days she has been in there in the trauma center.

The doctor, nurse and Jasper came into the room. Everyone looking at me as though I was the bad mother. I stepped aside so they could administer the sedative to calm her down. Jasper not knowing the whole truth of how she ended up here in the first place wanted to be by her side. I said, "No, she needs to cry, scream, whatever it took to get those emotions out before the meds kick in."

Because when the meds wear off there would be questions. More crying and probably screaming when I tell her that her precious and loving husband had cancelled his insurance policy two months prior to attacking her. According to the police report, the papers they found showed Dillon Mason had cancelled his insurance policy. All the passports had various last names so, they did a test and found he had no fingerprints or dental records they could use as identification. Only a driver license that showed Dillon Mason with my address.

A few hours later, Casper showed up with food, water, and a large coffee for me. An hour later, I went back to sit with Sky while she slept. The doctor came into the room, and I asked will she be ok and be able to remember?

He informed me she may have had some memory lost.

A few days later, the same detective was back, this time asking Sky questions about Dillon, about the guns, numerous passports in different names, and satchel of money found in the attic. After her response of no, no and no. He told her of their findings on him. His identity and his involved with various people,

Day 32

Sky was released from the hospital. We had no place to go as the police still had the yellow tape across the door and informed me it was still a crime scene. He suggested the names of companies that clean up crime scenes, and they are paid by the city in which the crime occurred. Until it happened to me, I never knew of their existence.

Chapter Thirty-One

I phoned Casper and inquired if he knew where we should go. He suggested we head north for a few days and contact my insurance company as they would provide us a place to stay until my house was ready to move back into.

Six months later, we were moving back into the house. Most of the furniture was gone, new carpet was put in, and money from insurance company was in the mail.

Just being back in that house, which I no longer considered my home, had a horrific effect on me more than it did to Sky probably because of her memory lost.

Nevertheless, just being back where that dreadful night of horror started had not been a healthy situation for either of us. There were times I heard Sky crying or having a nightmare. Some nights, we both had nightmares, and I was sure about the same thing.

Immediately after moving back into the house, Sky and I both went to therapy. It had been a dramatic experience sharing our innermost thoughts with strangers. I want to believe it had help. But deep down, I felt it was not helping fast enough.

Sky mind and body had gone through all stages of grief. But I thanked God she was not in a state of depression. Thanks to Jasper being there I believe it helped her a lot to transition back to a normal life.

She still has questions I do not answer. I feel as her mom, the answers I give would only hurt and serve no real purpose. But as his wife, she has a right to ask. Maybe one day, the questions will stop. She was hurt from the inside out as this was her first experience in losing a loved one even if it was Dillon.

Even today, she looks sad and cries a lot. I ask no questions. I told her once, "When you cry it signifies that you are alive, it helps cleanse the soul, and God has shown you favor."

The only way I know to help my child is to be there and listen. Give advice when needed and talk when she is ready. I keep reassuring her that what happened is not her fault. For anybody to do what he did took some planning of hatred and pure evil.

After I met Dillon and been around him, I always felt a chill. I knew and could feel something was amiss but never would have expected this to happen. Never in a million years did I want to be right about having the devil in the bedroom.

Honor Your Past

and

Treasure What You Have Now

Chapter Thirty-Two

It is too late to undo what Dillon has done. All we can do is move forward and hope for the best. It's what I call one of life's many lessons. Failure or quitting was never an option for Sky or myself. We continue to strive forward, hope for the best, stay in prayer and faith.

I constantly remind both of us we are still here.

Sky is still a beautiful young woman with a beautiful spirit. She has put her designer clothes, jewelries, and furs in various consignment stores and, with the monies she received, returned to school, working on her degree.

Jasper is still around and back in her life.

Now this one, Jasper Singleton, I have always approved of, and one day hope when all is well with her, they can make plans to move forward and make a life together. Maybe somewhere tropical so Mom can visit.

It has been nine years since that tragic event in our lives. I am diagnosed with sever PTSD (up till that night, I never heard of PTSD) and clinical depression. It is taken me longer to get over the tragedy of that one night. I am still in therapy and working on designing a blueprint for my life. I know it is going to take time, but I am getting there.

Oh yeah, Casper is still with me and ask me to marry him.

Acknowledgments

I am thankful to God for not allowing Sky to look back on that night. For giving us another chance at life and make a new start. For personally given me a chance to get closer to Him.

To my daughter, Sky, for being brave. For having the will to survive the tragedy and lost. To not let what happened determine or define who you are. Sweetie you made up your mind what you wanted out of life, went for, and achieved it. I am so immensely proud of you. Watching you smile helps remind me that life can be beautiful and that beauty of oneself is so precious.

Jasper, my dear sweet son, thanks for dropping everything to be here for Sky. You never talked about it, but I know you quit your job to be here just as I know you had another life and gave it all up just to be near Sky, and I love you for it. I will never forget what you said: ***"Moms, she is in a coma, but her breath is minty fresh."***

To my sister, Phoenix, for being there and never wavering. Even when I pushed you away, you would not go. You will always be my person. Do not ever change, for I would have no one to turn to in my time of need. Thanks for taking over when I could not and the numerous calls you made. You did a great job of taking care of me when I needed you. Thank you.

To La'niece and Melanie for being my prayer warriors and looking after us both when I could no longer stand alone to fight this battle. You will forever remain in my heart. I love you both.

Casper, from the day we met, you said you would never leave me, and you have proven yourself to be true. You came into my life unexpectedly, and I am so glad you did. And yes, you are still adorable, and I treasure our friendship forever and always. So, if you ask me again, I will say yes to be Mrs. Casper Dupont.

And to you, Dillon Mason, if you had not been so evil, I would not know how strong my faith, belief, and my own strength as a mother. Because of you, I am closer to God than before. May you rest in hell.

Before that terrible night, I thought I knew how to pray, but I did not. I have learned to humble myself before the Lord and have created my own prayer room. I daily give praise and seek guidance and understanding of His Word. I thank give thanks for having motherly instincts, and power to trust my judgment. Yes, I now wear a robe and preach HIS Word.

9 781664 175662